Negotiating a Historically White University While Black

By

Jack L. Daniel

Negotiating a Historically White University While Black

Jack L. Daniel

Published by:
Jack L. Daniel

Typesetting: Nicole Johnson, Digital Made Simple, LLC

Cover Design: Nicole Johnson, Digital Made Simple, LLC

A CIP record for this book is available from the Library of Congress Cataloging-in-Publication Data
Library of Congress Control Number: 2018912769

ISBN-13: 978-1-7324339-0-8

Printed in USA by Amazon

Dedication:

In remembrance of my mother and father, Grace C. and Russell P. Daniel as well as my mother and father-in-law Jerlean J. and Nathaniel S. Colley Sr. —essential souls who believed in and delivered me.

Contents

FOREWORD

It is not difficult to identify acts of overt racism in America today. They are blaring and clear violations of civil and human rights. Unfortunately, as a nation our attention is so focused on mitigating overt racism that we ignore micro-aggressions against people of color —acts of racism that are equally as damaging but harder to identify because they operate within the law. NEGOTIATING A HISTORICALLY WHITE UNIVERSITY WHILE BLACK unpacks many of the difficulties awaiting a person of color in academic spaces, allowing the reader to experience the types of micro-aggressions that subtly maintain a "Whites only" culture within academia.

Jack L. Daniel gives a face and a voice, sometimes via humor, other times via heartbreak, to the African American experience in historically White institutions of higher education. It is an honest, self-reflective autoethnographic narrative that is thought provoking and timely, challenging African American students to take responsibility for their own pursuit of excellence while at the same time challenging faculty and administrators to play their roles in insuring equal education access and success.

I have known Jack since my childhood and am one of the many beneficiaries of his contributions to the University of Pittsburgh and to African American students over his tenure there. It is my honor to recommend this book for personal gain or as a complementary text in an academic setting.

— Stacy Johnson, MAT

Stacy Johnson is a retired K–20 teacher after having taught over twenty years. Currently she is a doctoral student at The University of Texas at San Antonio focusing on Instructional Coaching and decolonizing pedagogical praxis.

PREFACE

"Driving while Black" underscores the adverse consequences that could befall a driver profiled by a police officer on the basis of the driver's race. Today, racism is so rampant that the phrase has been extended to other situations as in the cases of [1] "Waiting to order coffee while Black," i.e., six police officers arrested two Black men while they were waiting to order coffee at Starbucks; and [2] "Napping in a historically White university dorm lobby while Black," i.e., a White Yale student called police after observing a Black Yale student sleeping in the dormitory lounge. The following personal narrative presents the dynamics of my journey while being a Black student, faculty member and administrator in the historically White University of Pittsburgh.

As a Black male who began life in a section of Johnstown, Pennsylvania's segregated public housing while being parented by a working poor mother and father, I could have easily floated along the "school-to-prison" pipeline, become a name on the Viet Nam Memorial Wall, or, at best, a low-wage laborer drifting from job to job in a small town. Instead, a superficial glance at my educational background might suggest that I fit neatly into the mainstream narrative of the American Dream, i.e., the Horatio Alger myth holding that anyone can work hard and succeed.

A closer look at my educational journey, however, reveals the nearly miraculous way a Black, male, disadvantaged student negotiated a very complex labyrinth, i.e., negotiating a historically White University while Black. To be sure, there were times that

I did the essential hard work associated with achievement. To be equally sure, none of it would have been possible without fortuitous formal and informal interventions.

For more students such as myself to succeed in higher education, we cannot depend on the rather serendipitous factors that enabled me to succeed. Thus, my hope is that the telling of my story, covering a period of more than 40 years at the University of Pittsburgh, will aid those who wish to pro-actively assist Black students, faculty and administrators as well as other people of color prosper in historically White universities. Hence, with the intent of aiding those today who are focused on matters related to diversity, inclusion, equity and social justice, I offer constructive commentary which they might use to better their programs.

Acknowledgements

For the enduring inspiration they provide, this work is dedicated to [1] my grandchildren Akili, Amani, Deven and Javon; and [2] their parents, Anthony and Marijata Echols, Omari and Cherice Daniel, who serve as their primary navigators for assisting them with negotiating historically White educational systems.

As with other significant events in my life, Jerlean Evelyn Colley Daniel has been my muse for the past 55 years. As I prepared this manuscript, she read, re-read, and read again this manuscript. Her comments were critical to its completion.

My son, Omari C. Daniel, provided not only copy editing but also critical commentary and constructive criticism that significantly improved the content.

Dee Lawrence helped me to not have a "baptism by fire" when it came to navigating the contemporary world of publishing. Her freely given consultation paved the way for the final production of this book.

In a very supportive way, Nicole Johnson, Owner, Digital Made Simple, LLC designed the cover and formatted the text for publication.

It was an extremely challenging sojourn from an academically high-risk freshman to a Vice Provost, Dean, and Distinguished Service Professor. However, "what's hard to bear is sweet to remember." Therefore, as my mama Grace C. Young Daniel would say, "From the bottom of my heart," I thank those who helped me complete my course. Those University of Pittsburgh affiliated persons who enabled me are too many to list herein, but among them are the following who proved to be of critical importance: Professor Edwin Black, Provost Emeritus Donald M. Henderson, Provost Emeritus James V. Maher, Professor Jack Matthews, Chancellor Emeritus Mark A. Nordenberg, and Pitt alumni Linda Wharton Boyd, Imelda Bruce, Gil Duncan IV, Stacy Johnson, and Francine McNairy.

I thank the 1969 Black Action Society leaders who supported my first administrative appointment as the Interim Director of Black Studies. Finally, I offer a shout out to those sturdy Black bridges who aid current students through the work of the Pitt African American Alumni Council.

Jack L. Daniel

CHAPTER ONE:

The Mis-educated Child

The 1983 film, "All the Right Moves," featured a Polish high school football player, his peers, and others desperately trying to escape a small, failing, steel town. Because it was a small, depressed, coal mining and steel producing town, Johnstown, Pennsylvania was selected as an ideal place for filming. Long before the filming of "All the Right Moves," I had personally experienced the severe limitations of Johnstown's nurturing.

Only the few local White leaders such as the mayor, police chief, and descendants of local businessmen escaped the travails of growing up in my small isolated home town in which most people were going nowhere in life. Most of the doctors, dentists, and other professionals came from elsewhere. The other Whites I knew were working-poor living from paycheck to paycheck. They came from what they called their "old country," had weak commands of English, spoke fragments of Italian, German, or Polish, and had not graduated from high school. Many of the steel workers and coal miners suffered from Black Lung and other serious respiratory diseases as a result of inhaling unfiltered cigarettes and mill soot. With the exception of one Black dentist and a female mortician, those holding professional status in the community were primarily White males.

Like many other Black families that migrated north in search of alternatives to the miseries of southern racial segregation and the poverty associated with subsistence farming, my parents, Russell P. and Grace C. Daniel, initially found temporary housing with relatives in Conemaugh, a small town in Western Pennsylvania adjacent to the Bethlehem Steel Mill. They endured a harsh environment in which local roof tops, parked cars, and the small Conemaugh River were coated by rust brown pollutants that poured from the Mill's smoke stacks. After a year of sharing their relatives' residence, my parents moved into one of Johnstown's public housing units.

Possessing little more than grade school educations in the presence of widespread racial segregation, my parents' life outcomes were severely limited. My father worked on the local railroad, receiving the lowest wages for his manual labor. My mother's wages were, as she often stated, "five dollars a day and bus fare" for the sporadic domestic work she did while raising her five children.

My parents were masters of demonstrating how "enough could be as good as a feast" when it came to stretching scarce dollars budgeted for food. We children visited doctors only when something such as appendicitis or pneumonia threatened our lives. Mama delivered four of her five children at home. Daddy prepared "down home cures" for the common cold, fevers, and an array of aches and pains. Despite these and other severe adversities, my parents maintained a nurturing home environment, and they never lost hope for their children in the midst of despair.

Determined that their children would not repeat the cycle of poverty experienced by so many of their neighbors' children, my parents consistently advised us, "If you don't do anything else, get a good education so that you can go further in life than we did. God willing, go to college and make something of yourself." They emphasized the importance of good school decorum, following teachers' instructions, and always doing our best academically. In addition, they found ways to keep us engaged in constructive activities at home and in the community.

Notwithstanding the opportunity gaps faced by me and my siblings, unlike the vast majority of our Black peers, each of us found the support we needed to transcend the adverse circumstances in which we found ourselves. Briefly, my oldest brother, Russell, participated in the Boy Scouts and various school clubs, sang on our church choir, and, most importantly, consistently earned honor roll grades. Helped by a merit scholarship, loans, summer jobs, and the mentoring he received while attending the historically Black Lincoln University, he enjoyed a long career as a math teacher in the Philadelphia Public Schools.

After finishing high school, my older brother, Sterlin, had his Army tour of duty cut short by a tank injury that left him with a permanent disability in one arm. As a disabled veteran, the federal government provided him with support to enroll in the Williamsport Technical Institute where his emphasis was architectural drafting. He held his first full-time job with a Washington D. C. architectural firm and, subsequently, he became a registered architect.

My younger sister, Phillis, and brother, Stephen, had the critically important support of their older siblings as well as their parents. Phillis was an honor student throughout public school; earned a baccalaureate and master's degree; and served as a registered nurse before enjoying a long career in real estate. Stephen earned his baccalaureate, had a prosperous career with a major auto corporation and, subsequently, became a Baptist minister and a bank administrator.

Neither my parents' teachings nor older brothers' positive examples were sufficient cause for me to perform well academically. From the very beginning, I was a class clown and academic underachiever. Ironically, my negative behavior was, in part, a function of the fact that, before we entered school, my mother taught her children to recite the alphabet; print their names, telephone number and address; count to one hundred; and recite numerous Bible passages. She also taught me so well to read several pages of the first-grade vocabulary book that I still recall the following: Page One: "Me, See, Am, Man, Can." Page Two: "Is, In, It, At, To." Page Three: "My, You, On, Her, Run." Since my first-grade work was so easy and/or boring, I regularly played in the classroom.

What I viewed as a dreary home life also contributed to my playing at school. We Daniel children were not allowed to "run the streets all hours of the night." Mama and Daddy imposed a six p.m. curfew until we were old enough to obtain part-time evening jobs. Once we were home, my parents expected us to do homework; read the Bible; or perform household chores. Throughout my grade school years, there was neither a record player nor a television in our home. The small radio we owned was used primarily by my father to obtain local news and weather reports. We heard so many painful discussions regarding unpaid bills that it seemed as though our lives would never improve, that we were somehow doomed. With so much unpleasantness at home and given the lack of challenging academic experiences, school became my playground.

Initially, I simply played for the pure pleasure it gave without giving any thought to being disruptive. However, by the third grade, my poor classroom decorum and low academic performance placed me among the Yellow Birds, the lowest academically tracked group. Everyone knew that the highest performing group was the White Birds, followed in descending ability levels of Blue, Red, and Yellow Birds. To make matters worse, I faked a stuttering problem in order to spend more time during the day in a predominantly Black "special education" class with a close friend who stuttered.

Once in the section for students with learning disabilities, I faked my speech impediment so well that stuttering became integral to my normal way of talking. It was not until mid-year that I increasingly forgot to stutter and answered questions correctly to which I had previously given wrong answers. Then the learning specialist and teacher agreed to move me to the Red Birds. Despite this advancement, I persisted in acting like a "Dodo bird" throughout my formative school years. In addition, I had not one whit of racial consciousness. In fact, my racial consciousness was so misguided that one might have thought Carter G. Woodson had someone like me in mind when he wrote, The Miseducation of the Negro in 1933.

Often referenced as the "Father of Black History," Woodson maintained that a good education consisted of more than the acquisition of facts. It should also include an understanding of one's history and culture. Without the latter, Woodson concluded that a person would be mis-educated, prepared to work for others instead of self, and remain in the service of those responsible for the miseducation. In short, miseducation was a form of oppression that Woodson described as follows:

> ...*The problem of holding the Negro down, therefore, is easily solved. When you control a man's thinking you do not have to worry about his actions. You do not have to tell him not to stand here or go yonder. He will find his "proper place" and will stay in it. You do not need to send him to the back door. He will go without being told. In fact, if there is no back door, he will cut one for his special benefit...*

Since the responsibility for educating the Negro was in the wrong (White) hands, Woodson noted that the Negro knew nothing of and/or had disdain for things such as African or Negro History, Art, Literature, or scientific achievements. Mis-educated Negroes eagerly learned European languages, and, simultaneously, easily adopted the racist beliefs that African slaves spoke a savage gibberish, that there was no such thing as African languages. They believed all great music came from Europe, and had no appreciation for the Negro spiritual, blues, or any other art form of African origins. Most importantly, mis-educated Negroes never conceived of owning businesses, controlling their schools, or doing anything else for their collective advancement. Instead, they remained in roles designated by their masters, performing the hardest forms of manual labor and having no expectations for improving their miserable lots. By the time my miseducation had been completed, I was well conditioned to stay in societal designated places such as a laborer in the local steel mill, or a foot soldier in the Army.

My early childhood miseducation was reinforced both by what we learned and did not learn in our public schools with a vast majority White student body and all White professional staffing. I will never forget the time our White first grade teacher read the story of "Little Black Sambo" to our class. Most of the students, including me, laughed heartily at the dark-black, big-lipped, big-eyed, little boy who hysterically ran from the tiger. We were just children after all and this was much like the cartoons we loved. After school, in the absence of the White students, we mockingly called each other Little Black Sambo. During the short fifteen-minute walk home, two fist fights began and ended over who among us looked most like Little Black Sambo.

Members of my fifth-grade class snickered during a geography lesson covering Bunga and Simba, two dark-skinned African youths who wore next to nothing because it was so hot in their country. They lived in what looked like mud and straw huts as opposed to the suburban home I associated with Dick, Jane, and their dog Spot or the public housing I knew so well.

I was embarrassed by the Africans' nappy hair full of red mud which, as we were told, they believed to be decorative. My miseducation included my home community's view that good hair was long and straight, best exemplified by Whites. Bad hair was our nappy hair which could only be helped by the application of harsh chemicals followed by thick grease and the use of hot straightening combs.

My White geography teacher added to my miseducation by stating that Bunga and Simba were primitive children who could not speak English and, according to her, their few words for "hello" and "goodbye" sounded much like the stereotypical phrase, "mumbo-jumbo." It was not until I was an adult, far removed from Johnstown, that I learned "Hujambo" was the Swahili word for "hello," and that the African continent was one of the most multi-linguistic places in the world.

Our sixth grade American History material included a short section on the African slave trade. Instead of learning about the horrors of slavery, we were taught a good bit about how, like European immigrants, Africans ultimately benefited from being in America. We learned that these lowly dark-skinned people got rid of their savage gibberish and, with limited mental ability, acquired what little they could of English. We were taught that many replaced their heathen religions with Christianity.

Instead of references to slaves, the Africans were more often portrayed as people who quite willingly became good domestic servants and farmers, possessing some of the very best cotton-picking skills. We were told that these Africans displayed a jovial nature and were happy to entertain plantation owners and their friends with rhythmical singing and primitive dancing. We did not learn that this behavior perhaps reflected the resiliency of their human spirit to repression.

We grade school children heard plenty about the pilgrims and other European immigrants who came to America and allegedly lifted themselves up by their bootstraps. We received numerous examples of thrifty White men who explored the world in the process of discovering America, hard working men who subsequently became captains of industry, founders of colleges, ministers, Constitution authors, and leading politicians. We did not learn upon whose shoulders they climbed to achieve their success, whose land they stole, whose free labor drove their economy, and whose gods they supplanted.

The movies supplemented my teachers' miseducation process by presenting all White cowboys who conquered the wild Native American-infested west by driving out the "savages" and building booming towns. Sadly, back then, I believed the Native Americans were better than Blacks when it came to resisting oppression. Even though they ultimately were placed on reservations, the movies presented them as brave warriors who fought the White man and won some battles. I was proud of Chiefs Geronimo and Sitting Bull, but had never heard of Gabriel Prosser, Denmark Vesey, or any other slave revolt leader. For all I knew, Africans had simply acquiesced to the horrors of slavery.

The big screen also presented beautiful Native American women with long straight hair and, occasionally, a White man fell in love with one of them. In addition, the Native Americans had their own leaders, languages, tribes, and territories. They seemed to have so much going for them that, like many other ignorant Blacks ashamed of their African ancestry, I too sometimes claimed to be part-Indian.

Tarzan and Jane tried often but could do little to civilize the dark inhabitants of the African jungles. The movies made it clear that the buxom Jane Russell and Marilyn Monroe were love goddesses; there were no Black counterparts. It was movie manufactured common knowledge that the good guys wore white hats, good women were as pure as the fresh white snow, and little white lies were excusable. Complementing that mass mediated epistemology was the equating of black with evil as evidenced by black cats, black sheep of the family, blacklists, black ball, and the licentious behaviors of black people.

We did not learn about Harlem Renaissance writers or any other strides of Black culture that were occurring in more sophisticated parts of the country outside of Johnstown, Pennsylvania. Never once did a teacher or anyone else mention historical figures such as Frederick Douglass or Sojourner Truth. Black history began with slavery. Africa, to me, was a dark and dangerous continent. There simply was nothing, while I was growing up, that provided any kind of positive reinforcement for being African or Black. A childhood incident summarizes the mentality that we shared regarding being Black.

A "teasing-tan" ten-year-old Rusty Jefferson said my father was black. A few kids laughed and, after I told my parents, a Daniel-Jefferson family feud lasted throughout the summer. My mother and Mrs. Jefferson ceased speaking to each other, the children were not allowed to play together, and it took a family meeting to end the matter. Mr. Jefferson apologized on behalf of his family, but the formerly friendly family relationships were never the same.

Long before the first signs of puberty, "high yellow," "teasing tan," "golden honey," and white were my as well as my male friends' preferred colors for ideal females. I desired no girl darker than a brown paper bag, even though I knew nothing of the so-called "no darker than a brown paper bag" test some middle-class Blacks used as the litmus test for including people in their social circles. Having internalized so much racism related to our physiology, we high school students readily quipped, "If you're white, you're all right. If you're yellow, you're mellow. If you're brown, stick around. But if you're black, get back."

Properly mis-educated, I evolved into the consummate clown, the well-known junior high school jerk who threw sal ammoniac into a Bunsen burner, resulting in so much chemically-laced smoke that the building had to be evacuated. My reputation as a maladjusted student was sealed when I was identified as a key participant in the senior high school illegal lottery based on the principal's end of the day announcements which included the daily absentee rates. Had it not been for my parents' excellent reputation, the principal might not have agreed for my parents to essentially keep me under house arrest.

Today, the process of miseducation continues because many Blacks attend segregated public schools that are truly separate and unequal, schools where the majority of the students fail to achieve basic skills required for graduation, schools where they perform several years below their grade levels. In most instances, the curriculum contains a sprinkling of "Black History" courses as electives. Quite often, students are dependent upon a single informed teacher to add a Black-authored book to the required courses. At the same time, significant numbers of parents want Nobel Prize-winning Toni Morrison's The Bluest Eye banned from the high school curriculum.

With education truly being the "passport for the 21st century," few things are more important for Black student academic success than sustained efforts to closing the "opportunity gap" in order to close the often referenced "achievement gap." As Jerlean E. Daniel noted in a May 2018 special issue of Young Children,

> ...opportunity gap captures those policies and practices that trap far too many children in a downward spiral. In some communities that have been starved for resources across generations, there truly does appear to be a cradle-to-prison pipeline. Specifically, children of color from low-oncome families typically attend under-resourced schools and live in under-resourced neighborhoods. They are disproportionately penalized in a climate of zero tolerance and more often than not, they are viewed as having an array of cultural and cogni-

tive deficits. While their personal and cultural strengths are unrecognized or ignored...

As it truly "takes a village to raise a child," it is also of critical importance that members of the emerging Black middle class "lift as they climb" by serving as mentors who expose Black students to careers beyond sports and entertainment. The motivational effect could be as profound as when the two-year-old Black child was photographed while she was fascinated by the portrait of Michele Obama and, after Michele Obama met with her, sent the message,

> *Keep on dreaming big for yourself ... and maybe one day I'll look up proudly at a portrait of you.*

CHAPTER TWO:

The Low Risk

At the beginning of my 1960 senior year in high school, there was not one iota of evidence to suggest that the American social mobility dream was a possibility for me. There were few routes for Blacks to escape the stifling impact of poverty, limited education, inadequate health care, and Johnstown's racist employment practices that relegated us to low level labor positions. I did not have the talent to become an acclaimed athlete, a famous soul singer, a rhythmical dancer or any other stereotypical role reserved for Blacks in the entertainment world.

Having succumbed to the lore of low academic achievement being synonymous with Black masculinity, my inferior high school transcript rendered me inadmissible to college. This dysfunctional mentality also led me to view military service as my postsecondary "reach school," the local Bethlehem Steel Mill as my "safe school," and hustling for tips at Jolly Joe's Carwash as my "no more school" scenario. Fortunately, I never had to pursue any of these options.

One evening after a spring track practice, my tired feet had barely passed through the door before my father gave me his no nonsense look and told me that I was scheduled to meet with the President of the University of Pittsburgh at Johnstown (UPJ). Startled, I asked, "For what?" Daddy replied sternly, "Now you listen to me good! Some important people might be able to help you better yourself. You put on your best church clothes, go out to the college, and meet with the President next Tuesday at 9 a.m. Do just what he tells you, whatever that might be. If he admits you, then some downtown business people are going to put up enough money for a half scholarship. You let me worry about the rest of the money, and I'll speak to your teachers about you missing school that morning."

I complied with Daddy's orders, and there I stood outside the UPJ President's office, posing in the most hypocritical fashion as a deserving student seriously interested in acquiring a college education. My horrendous Scholastic Aptitude Test (SAT) combined score of 810, barely passing grades, fourth-fifth high school rank, negative disposition toward the formal schooling process, and delinquency problems provided no reasonable expectation for me to attend college. There was a greater chance of hitting the daily number that so many neighborhood poor people played illegally. Still, I desired the glory of telling people I had been admitted to UPJ as opposed to being seen as one of the misfits who had yet to declare what they would do after high school graduation.

Knowing that there was no academic reason for me to be admitted much less receive a scholarship made me so apprehensive that a pervasive fear of being rejected engulfed me. Cold sweat began to drip from my armpits and slowly slide down my sides as I anticipated what the UPJ President might ask me. My hands shook so much that I sought control by stuffing them into my pants' pockets. Then I did my best to gather myself by standing still for a few moments and clearing my dry throat.

As soon as I entered the President's office, a woman looked up from her typewriter, squinted her bluish green eyes, and rather dryly asked, "May I help you find where you're going?"

Certain that I had seen "Office of the President" written boldly on the door, but lacking confidence, I sheepishly told her that I was looking for the President's office.

A bit puzzled, the secretary asked, "Yes, but to whom do you want give whatever you came to deliver?"

Stammering a bit, I responded, "My, my, father said that, that he and some, some other people wanted me to meet with the President."

Still displaying considerable doubt, she demanded, "What is your name and what are you to deliver?"

Dismayed, I meekly mouthed, "Jack Daniel."

Upon hearing my name, she sighed, "Oooooh! So, you're one of them. I heard about this experimental whatever. Just a minute and I'll let the President know that you're here."

The reference to one of them was not too different from you people, an expression that many Blacks viewed as a euphemism for nigger. A lifetime of training to respect elders plus the prospect of a special admission to UPJ helped me to suppress the anger, but not the deep emotional hurt, that now added to my initial anxiety. Similar to the experiences of so many other educationally disadvantaged, high risk, or special-admit students of color entering historically White campuses through some euphemistically titled program, it took only a few insensitive words from a lower level institutional representative to nearly dash the tiny glimmer of hope that flickered within me regarding becoming a college student.

The secretary knocked softly on the President's highly polished oak door, an authoritative voice answered "Yes," and she entered slowly closing the door behind her. Returning a few minutes later, she uttered a curt, "The President will be with you shortly." "Shortly" turned out to be approximately thirty minutes and, during that time, only my father's orders to attend the meeting prevented me from leaving. With this initial half hour wait and similar events over time, it became increasingly clear that I was to always be on time, and never have the expectation of reciprocation. Only a lack of appreciation for the special institutional things being done for me as well as other defects in my character could permit me to be impatient.

A half bald, short, man finally appeared in the doorway of his office. He reminded me of the White men who lived across the street from us in our racially segregated projects, the only differences being his dark blue suit, white shirt and a tie instead of their plaid shirts and tattered blue denim jeans. Standing in the doorway of his office, the President looked over at me and inquired, "Are you prepared to attend a very good college?" I said, "Yes sir," putting an emphasis on the "sir" as my parents had trained me to do when responding to adults. Then he beckoned for me to come into his office, turning away before I had gotten out of my chair.

Before I got close enough to shake his hand, the President turned, picked up some papers, and asked me to sit on a sofa across from the huge desk on which he sat. Hoping he had not seen my extended hand, I sat quickly. Then, he stood, folded his hands behind his back in a drill sergeant fashion, and silently stared down at me for what seemed an interminable time. I couldn't determine if he were assessing my body, my character, another aspect of my being, or something that had nothing to do with me. When I looked above the bifocals on his nose and briefly peeped into his light blue eyes, he began talking in a voice suggestive of a stern warning.

"Look, we're going to give you a mighty big chance, a second chance to make something of yourself. I know your high school record is not worth much, but I and some important people want to help you, boy." Then he picked up a stack of papers, disgustingly flipped through several pages, stopped at one, and added, "I see here that you have a pretty poor SAT score, you're ranked near the bottom of your class, you had some conduct problems, and you didn't take a very challenging curriculum. What was going on with you, boy?"

Cold sweat again began to drip from my armpits, a strong urge to urinate made itself known to me, my breathing became difficult, and, unable to fathom a response, I sheepishly stared at him. Disgust, signified by an increasing reddish hue, caused the President to breathe a bit heavily as he asked in a chastising fashion, "How could you perform so poorly after being raised in such a good family?"

Unable to fathom a response as my ego begged for a defense, I hung my head. Daddy was the epitome of the hard working, fundamentalist Baptist deacon, the proud Prince Hall mason, and the tireless community leader who consistently advised me and other youth to "make something" of ourselves by getting a good education. Mama was the quintessential, dutiful wife, and nurturing mother who also stressed the value of education, along with what she termed a "good heart." Yet I exemplified what my parents deemed "hard-headed," their child who Mama said "had to be burned before he believed the stove was hot."

I finally mustered the excuse of having had to financially help my family by working in the bowling alley, setting pins from 7:30 to 10 on school nights. In my most pitiful voice, I said, "I didn't make much, but the ten or twelve dollars a week paid for my school lunches and helped with bread, milk and other groceries. Those late hours of hard work, along with running cross-country in the fall and track in the spring left me too tired and without enough time to study."

Seemingly not very impressed, the President responded, "Well, as I said, we know your parents are very good people. Plus, you won't be working in September or playing sports. Therefore, we're going to take you this semester and, if you somehow, for reasons known only to God, earn at least a 'C' average for two terms, then you can stay. Now, this isn't something that you need to go discussing with others. You just show up in September and make your folks, other good colored people, and the rest of us proud of you. Do you think you can do that?"

With the small amount of confidence that I could generate, I nodded my head and replied with a weak "Yes, sir." Then the President removed any remaining doubts regarding what he thought of me attending UPJ when he warned, "Just remember that you must somehow manage to keep a 'C' average for two terms or we will have to let you go. There won't be any more second chances! Frankly, I'm not sure of why some folks want to go through all of this with you and that other kid, but we'll see, we'll see. College is college, not some social program!"

With that, he stood up, gave me an envelope, and told me to take it down the hall to my advisor who would assist me with class selections. He was through, there was no more to be said, and I left with my head hung low, noticing only the secretary's feet while passing her desk.

"Social program" and "welfare" were very negative things to me and my family members, especially my mother who was very proud of our family having never been on welfare. We children heard so many times about how we were better than other poor people when, after some sort of family financial crisis, my mother offered, "At least we didn't have to go on welfare like those other folks." Government-provided surplus cheese, flour and butter were not to be found in our home. No matter what we didn't have, we always had something to eat, clean clothing, and a clean home. Daniels didn't depend on handouts. Yet, now I stood alone in a college building's hallway having been deemed essentially a welfare recipient.

I left the President's office and meandered to the advisor's office where I met a thin, middle-aged White man who looked as though he barely weighed enough to be a featherweight on my high school wrestling team. He had a few gray hairs, and spoke with a very soft, almost childish voice. After receiving his extremely limp and cold clammy handshake, it quickly became clear that he too had a concern with me becoming a UPJ student.

As soon as I said, "I'm Jack Daniel and I'm here to register," my advisor stated, "Well now, I've heard about you." Next, he repeated what I would hear over and over in various forms for many years to come, "You should consider yourself quite fortunate." Then, reminding me of the goodness of my benefactors, he added, "Those are some really neat people and this is a mighty fine institution to be giving you this chance." Until my advisor spoke, I had naively thought no one at the college other than the President and his staff knew about my special admission and scholarship.

Turning to the purpose of our meeting, my advisor asked, "What are your interests, now that you're here?"

Without hesitating, I replied truthfully, "card playing, women, and fishing."

A big frown came over his reddened face and he mumbled, "I see where this conversation is headed."

When the advisor offered me a choice between Physical Education and Air Force ROTC, I immediately chose Air Force ROTC believing the Air Force to be a solid career back up plan, just in case the "C" average proved elusive over the next two terms. My experience was that primarily high achieving White students joined the Air Force, those with athletic inclinations became Marines, and, mostly

Blacks and poor Whites signed up with the Army which enlisted practically anyone who could "shoot and salute." I also had two older, high achieving friends who entered the Air Force and moved up in rank. Should I fail at UPJ, I thought I would stand a better chance of following in their footsteps.

After making my ROTC choice, my advisor asked no further questions. He too seemed to know what was best for me, and he proceeded to fill out the rest of my course schedule. He uttered not one word about graduation requirements, distribution of studies requirements, selecting majors, or any other academic regulations. He simply registered me for a typical first semester set of classes including an elementary course in English Composition, Spanish, Air Force ROTC, Psychology, and Biology, handed me the form, and, in a voice much more like an order than a request, said, "Sign where I placed the check mark." I pretended to scan the form and quickly signed. After he too signed, the advisor told me to take the form to the Registrar's Office.

I had never heard of a Registrar's Office and was too embarrassed to ask anything about its function. Fortunately, after taking only a few steps down the hall, I saw the title on a door. Once inside the office, a young White woman behind the counter quickly said, "Over here, please." I hesitated and she quickly inquired, "You're Jack Daniel, aren't you?" Dumbfounded by the fact that she too knew something about me, I offered no verbal response and simply handed her the registration form.

As the woman's eyes lingered on my list of courses, I could not determine if her issue was disbelief, dismay, disdain, all three, or something else. After a considerable pause and in a very authoritative voice, she said "You can just leave this slip with me. Your billing will be handled in a special fashion. That's it for today. If I were you, I'd get back here the first day of school and do as I'd been told." I said nothing and left the Registrar's office feeling increasingly concerned about all of the UPJ people who knew the compliant behavior that I should exhibit. One could ascertain from their comments that Jack Daniel was an outsider, an interloper, someone clearly not wanted and possibly despised, but nevertheless was being admitted to their fine institution.

During my bus ride home, I continued to dwell on the many ominous signs related to attending UPJ. "You people" and "social program" reverberated in my mind. My perception of an unfriendly and possibly hostile environment was reinforced by not having seen a single person of color throughout the morning. My schedule of classes made little sense to me. There was no clarity regarding how the second part of my bill would be paid, much less a source of funding for my books or the daily commute to and from UPJ. In addition, although I wanted the glory of telling my friends that I had been admitted to UPJ, my terrible high school performance caused me to vacillate. More required readings, papers to write, and final examinations were the very last things I wanted after getting out of high school.

I began to conjure up an escape plan. In September, maybe I would sign up for the Air Force, tell nobody, and write back from whatever military base to which I had been sent. A moment's reflection suggested that this was pure fantasy and, as the bus rumbled along, I began to rehearse a discussion that I would first have with my mother about the fact that UPJ was not the place for me. If she was sympathetic, then I would try an improved version with my more difficult father. However, knowing that it was nearly impossible to succeed with them, I quickly resigned myself to attending UPJ for at least one trial semester.

The very next Sunday, I was energized about becoming a college student. During the testimonial part of our church service, Mama stood and then made me stand beside her. With one arm around my waist and crying tears of joy, she declared, "God is still on the throne! I'm so happy this morning! I'm so blessed that my son, Jack, is headed to college! Some of you know I've been so worried for him, but God's made a way for him to go to Pitt in September."

A close family friend, Ms. Lightfoot, screamed, "You're right Sis Daniel! God's still on the throne! Bless you and your child. Just goes to show, there's help for everybody."

Deacon Holmes added, "God bless that child," and then began an acapella version of "The Lord Will Make a Way Somehow."

The spirited singing gave way to frenzied shouting by the old saints. As the spirit possession spread, I could feel Mama's trembling body and some of her warm tears that fell on my hand. Overwhelmed by the church family's support, my body seemed to have become engulfed by a tremendous, heated, emotional rush and I too felt possessed. My knees buckled and my limp self slid into the pew. With my head bowed, I too cried joyously.

Later during the service, our minister indicated he would take up a special collection for me. When the money was counted, he announced a total of $35 and called me forward to receive the envelope. As he shook my hand and the church applauded, I finally received the confirmation my being so badly needed.

Years later, while recalling my first visit to UPJ, an undercurrent of guilt began to tug at me. A quick inspection of my courses taken and barely passing high school grades should have quickly led to my rejection. A simple check of the publicized Johnstown High School Honor Roll would have identified several Black students with significantly higher grades and related class rankings. Had they checked with Johnstown High School officials, they would have identified about a dozen much more qualified Black students to attend UPJ. Yet, based primarily on my parents' reputation, concern with integrating UPJ expressed by a local White community leader, and whatever motivations caused the UPJ President to admit me, I was provided a true chance of a lifetime.

When I asked my father why he was contacted regarding the possibility of me attending UPJ, he told me that a White store owner asked his Black janitor if he knew of any "worthwhile Negro children who deserved a chance to attend college." The janitor reportedly indicated that Deacon and Sister Grace Daniel were good church people, and he would check to see if they had a child graduating from high school. Fortunately for me, he did check and I received the special admission to UPJ. Although I never learned the store owner's identity, I remain forever grateful for his generosity at a time of my great need.

In retrospect, my admission to UPJ reminded me of some aspects of the biblical Moses story. UPJ was akin to Pharaoh's house because it was essentially an establishment institution that helped to maintain Johnstown's and the larger society's White male dominant social order and, therefore, it should have been the last place to provide a special opportunity for me. It had been "decreed" that I should drown in the sea of socially induced destruction that engulfed so many others. Instead, as in the case of baby Moses, a concerned member of the established order plucked me from the reed basket woven by my parents and saved me by assisting with my admission to UPJ. However, unlike the nurturing Moses consistently received from his mother while he was in Pharaoh's house, my alma mater (my "dear mother") neither provided individual nor institutional practices dedicated to nourishing my retention and graduation.

Instead of immediately assigning me to a faculty advisor who made it very clear to me that my academic success was of great importance to them and, therefore, they would consistently provide me with support, UPJ staff greeted me with admonishment and indifference. Had there been an institutional desire for me to succeed, I should have been given mandatory study hours. My faculty advisor should have closely monitored my performance in all classes and, in conjunction with my other instructors, developed academic interventions as required.

It was institutionally irresponsible for UPJ to define academic success, for me, as a "C" average when a "C" average was the thin line before crossing into failure. I had already cultivated a low aiming academic mentality and, absent a challenge, there was no reason for me to aim higher in terms of my academic performance. Instead of the UPJ administration reinforcing my counterproductive behavior by presenting me with low academic expectations, it should have been made clear to me that a "C" average was a requirement to avoid academic probation/suspension, but most definitely not a standard to which any student should aspire.

Given the way that I was quite literally left on my own to succeed academically, it was quite draconian for UPJ to admit me instead of others with much better academic records and a greater likelihood of succeeding without formal interventions. What better way to demonstrate the futility of a race-based special opportunity initiative than to enroll and not assist an educational misfit whose academic credentials indicated a very low probability of success? I was the precise person needed to enable a naysayer, after one semester, to say, "See, we gave one of 'those people' a chance, and look at how he squandered the opportunity."

Because I was admitted but never institutionally supported by UPJ, I have never been able to accept UPJ as my alma mater, my "dear mother." Why should a child love a mother who, at worst, was willfully neglecting or, at best, painfully indifferent when it came to providing the bare essentials for the child's survival?

In contradistinction to my disposition toward UPJ, note how in The Truth We Hold, Senator Kamala Harris described the beauty of her alma mater, Howard University.

> *Every signal told students that we could be anything--that we were young, gifted, and black and we shouldn't let anything get in the way of our success. ...We weren't just told we had the capacity to be great; we were challenged to live up to that potential!*

CHAPTER THREE:

Bridging the Gap

I looked forward to joining other high school seniors excitedly discussing their college choices. On the way to my gym class, I met my classmate Mike to whom a Big Ten college had offered a football scholarship. Full of pride, I exclaimed, "Hey, man. I was admitted to UPJ!"

Sarcastically, Mike asked, "Who'll be after you next, Harvard?" I answered quickly, "No, I'm not kidding. UPJ also gave me a scholarship." Before he could respond, our mutual friend Margaret joined us and inquired, "What's going on with you two?" Now laughing, Mike explained, "Jack says he getting a scholarship from UPJ. Can you believe this guy?" Margaret chimed in, "Sure, and last week he ran a really fast mile at practice. I checked, but no one knew about his great time."

My excitement blinded me from the realization that neither they nor any other Johnstown High School student had reason to believe any college would admit me, much less award a merit scholarship. Further confirmation of my widely-held negative image came when I ran into my gym teacher and said, "Mr. Jones, I got admitted to UPJ!" In a grouchy, please do not disturb me voice, he ordered, "Jack, get dressed and get out on the gym floor. And, don't fool around in the locker room!" Perhaps, his negative disposition was a precursor to the anger some display today toward what they perceived to be unjust "diversity" or "affirmative action" programs offered to undeserving students of color.

Even I began to wonder about my status when, unlike other college-bound students who were receiving piles of mail, no flurry of welcoming UPJ mail came to me. There was no notice of freshman orientation, and especially worrisome was the fact that I had not even received an admission letter. The President's reluctant verbal acknowledgement that I was being given a special opportunity and the wrinkled blue copy of my signed fall schedule constituted the only evidence of my UPJ admission.

Paranoia caused me to wonder if the UPJ administration had protected its institutional reputation by not keeping a record of my special admission, in the event that I turned out to be an abysmal academic failure. An even gloomier thought was that, on the grounds that I was never admitted, the administration had provided itself with a means to deny my diploma if I somehow succeeded academically. Daddy kept insisting that the UPJ President would keep his word, but my doubts persisted until he and Mama received a late June letter containing my tuition bill. Surely, I reasoned, the University would not bill them if I hadn't been admitted.

The long cover letter indicated that half of the $425 costs had been paid by my scholarship donor. With a much needed $100 gift from Daddy's Masonic lodge, my church's $35 donation, and promised help from my oldest brother, Russell, I didn't think there was much for which my parents had to fret. Russell Jr. had graduated from college, worked for a year, and was always very supportive of me.

Nevertheless, my parents continued what seemed like daily discussions of the possible ways to make the remaining fall term payments and how to pay for the second term. Mama volunteered that she could get by without the new winter coat she had postponed purchasing last year and then added, "We'll just have to go a little longer without buying a car." My ever-confident father replied, "Don't worry Grace. God will make a way, somehow and you will get your coat."

As they fretted, I experienced considerable guilt for adding to the family's already problematic financial circumstances. Recalling the many struggles to pay my older brothers' educational expenses and, again feeling somewhat unworthy of the UPJ opportunity, I began to wonder if I shouldn't postpone enrollment until I had worked and saved for a year.

I also found myself increasingly doubtful regarding my ability to cope academically at UPJ. How was I going to pass college-level English composition after barely squeezing by in high school English? Latin had been a joke, a class for which I received a passing grade for two notable accomplishments: playing a Roman warrior in a skit when no other guy would do so and clowning around wearing a toga at the Latin class party. Soon, I would be faced with learning Spanish. It would be a total and utter disaster if my family endured more fiscal hardships and I failed academically.

I was too embarrassed by my past academic performance to muster enough courage to ask any of my teachers or the guidance counselor about strategies for college success. Even worse, I didn't know what questions to ask them. I wasn't willing to disclose my anxieties to my older siblings for fear of appearing to be less than a strong man. My one hoped-for source of academic support emanated from the fact that my life-long best friend, George Joy, had been admitted to UPJ.

George came from a well-respected Black family headed by hard working parents who held offices in their A.M.E. Methodist church. They migrated from South Carolina, moved doors apart from us in public housing, and eventually moved to a private home. He and I were classmates from first through twelfth grade. Throughout senior high school, he was the better athlete earning school letters in wrestling, track, and cross country. I competed in cross country and track but failed to earn a letter in either. Academically, he performed at a solid "B+" level while I dwelled in the barely passing category. Other than his family's difficulty with paying tuition, George never expressed anxiety to me regarding succeeding at UPJ. My hope was that he would help me academically negotiate UPJ, just as he had often given me tips when we competed in athletics.

During the morning of the first day of classes, George suggested that we stop by the one-room bookstore. I agreed because I was very eager to purchase a UPJ hat, sweatshirt, or something to outwardly distinguish me from other local high school graduates who still lived at home and had not found a job, joined the military, or enrolled in college. However, cursory glances at the clothing and book price tags indicated that we clearly could not afford to purchase our required books, much less UPJ paraphernalia. Typical of his sense of humor, George pointed to one book's price and, imitating the singer Little Richard, exclaimed, "Good golly miss molly! Man, let's get out of here!"

We left the bookstore and walked over to the red brick, four-floor, former grade school building that served as UPJ's multi-purpose building. We entered the small student lounge where approximately 35 White students had assembled. Many of them stared as we slowly made our way across the room toward several vacant chairs.

Having just left empty-handed from the bookstore, I took envious note of the UPJ gear the students were wearing as well as their colorful book bags lined against the walls. Six or seven boisterous fraternity men, wearing white shirts emblazoned with red Greek letters, were gathered around a table. Nearby, another group of students clustered at a table spoke with accents suggesting that they were from New Jersey and/or New York. I listened as several older students uttered terms such as "Psych," "Poli-sci," "Organic," and "Stat" in reference to their fall classes. None of what I saw or heard suggested that I belonged in this not simply chilly but freezing campus climate.

Absent a freshman orientation and given the unfamiliar sights and sounds of the student lounge, a sense of being an alien engulfed me. The feeling worsened after I tried to interact with several National Honor Society students from my high school. My "please acknowledge me" smile was rebuffed by their quickly turned heads. When their eyes could no longer avoid mine, their facial expressions seemed to suggest their confusion stimulated by my presence. Eventually, we meandered over to two of my high school classmates, exchanged rather dry hellos, and having confirmed that no one was eager to have an extended conversation, George suggested that we go over and watch several card games that were in progress.

Two tables of guys and one of girls were playing Bridge which we quickly noted was similar to Bid Whist, a game as integral to my cultural experience as baseball was to the American baseball, hot dogs, and apple pie trilogy. A Bid Whist game or two could be found at any of my family's social gathering. Along with the actual card playing, the experience included hours of trash talking, storytelling, joking, drinking, eating hot fish sandwiches loaded with hot sauce and chasing them with ice-cold sodas and beer.

Noting the similarities between the two games, I perceived a potential entre to the UPJ White student community. At first glance, it seemed the much easier game because, as they bid, the Bridge players announced suits such as "one club," followed by "one diamond," "two hearts," "two spades," and "two no trump." Bid Whist players made one bid without announcing their intended trump suit. Quite interested in the new game, I asked one of the onlookers to explain a bid that took place. To my surprise, he and his friend offered to teach George and me by playing a game.

Little did I know that my learning to play Bridge would be far more than simply learning a new game, that it would be tantamount to being hit by what Ngugi wa Thiongo articulated as the "cultural bomb." In his <u>Decolonizing the Mind</u>, the Kenyan writer indicated,

> ...But the biggest weapon wielded and actually daily unleashed by imperialism ...is the cultural bomb. The effect of a cultural bomb is to annihilate a people's belief in their names, in their languages, in their environment, in their heritage of struggle, in their unity, in their capacities and ultimately in themselves. It makes them see their past as one wasteland of non-achievement and it makes them want to distance themselves from that wasteland...

In the African colonial context, the colonized people developed negative views toward African names and replaced them with "good" European names. European dress replaced traditional African clothing. African languages became secondary to European languages as the primary languages of the schools, judicial system, church, and all other important aspects of society. Deities such as

Ngai and Mumbi gave way to God and Jesus. Most important to this process of cultural annihilation is the fact that it takes place while the oppressed people are allegedly being enlightened but, in reality, are being prepared to better serve the colonizer, as was what began to happen to me as I learned to play Bridge.

Although I naively viewed it as something of my culture, I did not know that Bid Whist was a variant of Whist which was promulgated by the British several centuries ago. Originally played by all social classes, Whist evolved into the much more highly structured, rule-governed Bridge preferred by middle- and upper-class players. Bid Whist remained very popular among lower class Whites and Blacks.

In keeping with the race and class distinctions between Bridge and Bid Whist players, a different language and behavioral norms accompanied each game. For example, Bridge etiquette requires the players to engage in polite conversation and leave their cards on the table until the dealer has finished distributing them. Bid Whist players pick up their cards as they are dealt and, watching the suits develop in their hands, enthusiastically talk trash such as, "Just give me this one more card and you turkeys are going to take a serious whipping."

We Bid Whist players slammed winning cards on the table just as we slammed "bones" on the table when playing dominoes. Bridge players delicately placed their cards on the table. Instead of playing the last winning card on the table, an excited Bid Whist player might turn the card, face up, and slap it on their forehead. At most, a Bridge player would gently place the last winning card on the table and softly say, "Making four as bid."

A Bid Whist player "throws off" but a Bridge player "discards" a card when he or she doesn't have a suit and elects not to play a trump card. When a trump card is played, Bridge players use the term "rough" as opposed to the term "cut" used in Bid Whist. I experienced glares of disapproval the first time I played a trump card in Bridge and exclaimed loudly, "I'll cut that!"

Initially, I thought the loudness of my voice was the problem at the Bridge table. When I next used "cut" in a softer voice, the students' frowns suggested that it was more of a semantic issue.

Nevertheless, "rough" seemed to be far too pretentious. It took nearly a semester for me to comfortably say "rough" and, by then, I was rapidly falling victim to a "cultural bomb" –something that can happen so subtlety but quite significantly to Black students negotiating historically White universities.

I learned the language of Bridge and learned it well. What I also learned was aptly described in Frantz Fanon's <u>Black Skin, White Masks</u>. Fanon was born in Martinique, left to fight with the French during World War II, and then completed his medical and psychiatric education in France. His writing addressed the effects of colonialism and racism, with an emphasis on psychological disorders. He too focused on colonial languages' impact on the minds of its victims, noting specifically,

> *To speak means to be in a position to use certain syntax, to grasp the morphology of this or that language, but it means above all to assume a culture, to support the weight of a civilization. ...A man who has a language consequently possesses the world expressed and implied by that language ... the colonized is elevated above his jungle status in proportion to his adoption of the mother country's cultural standards. He becomes whiter as he renounces his blackness, his jungle.*

Slowly but surely, learning the language of Bridge contributed to my turning away from my "blackness," my "jungle." I increasingly looked forward to playing Bridge, and I gradually developed disdain for Bid Whist. My first love was not simply different. It increasingly seemed to be an inferior game of chance as compared to the more cerebral Bridge. After a semester of exposure, playing Bid Whist transitioned into something to be done only when I returned home and desired to show those "lesser educated" ghetto people that I could still "get down with the people."

As I sought to transition from the predominantly Black lower-class world of Whist to the predominantly high-White society of Bridge, it was inconceivable at the time to believe that I was doing anything but having fun. Indeed, I thought I was exploiting my opponents by playing penny-a-point games, often taking home a couple of dollars. My new income source was sufficient for me to periodically purchase a hot dog and a drink instead of eating the soggy, room temperature, baloney, mustard and hot sauce sandwiches from home. Additionally, by beating them at their own game, I thought I was making fools of those who initially rejected me. As things turned out, however, I was the victim undergoing an inappropriate significant shift in my cultural bearings.

The first inkling that something was awry came during the beginning of the second term at which time I told two White Bridge players that George and I wanted to teach them a game that was very similar to Bridge. After George explained the basic rules of Bid Whist, the two of them began laughing and refused to play. I reminded them of how we had learned to play Bridge, and eventually they agreed to try Bid Whist. Several other students, gathered around the table, giggled, and commented on "this new stupid game" being taught by George and Jack. George and I won three hands in a row at which time our opponents refused to play what they deemed an "utterly ridiculous" game.

The combination of our so easily opting to fit in by playing Bridge and their refusal to accept Bid Whist as a legitimate game reminded me of what happened when my church periodically met with a White church to demonstrate how well we Christians could rise above racial intolerance. When we visited the White congregation, our choir not only sang their favorite songs but also dropped our syncopated, hand clapping, rhythmical singing style. We even sang "I Surrender All," a song they loved and we seldom sang. Seemingly oblivious to the thought of accommodating us, they came to our church, sang songs from their standard repertoire, and never varied their style. They stayed within their culture even though they often said how much they loved the way we sang, how our singing style moved them so deeply and sparked their spirituality.

The foregoing primarily one-way flow of cultural exchange is typical of the cultural dynamics that Black students face on historically White campuses. So, for example, we went to their side and acquired what I had thought to be their utterly ridiculous

Bridge etiquette. However, much more transpired in terms of my cultural transformation.

For example, I had seldom read anything from the local daily paper. Within weeks of learning Bridge, I faked being an avid newspaper reader because so many of the good Bridge players regularly read various sections of the *New York Times* and the local paper. I began to read the Bridge columns, then the sports section and, subsequently, scanned the news. Instead of being silent as the Bridge cards were dealt, I increasingly engaged in the chit chat related to current events. Reading the news, no doubt helped me in terms of my overall growth and development but, in the UPJ context, my problem emanated from why I was reading the news.

My newspaper reading was nothing more than gaining social approval from White students. The fact that I enjoyed some of what I read was of little conscious consequence for me. Most importantly in terms of the negative values placed on aspects of my culture, I would not have dared to tell the White students about something I had read in a Black newspaper such as the *Pittsburgh Courier*, which was available in our local barber shops.

It didn't take long for me to realize that discussing the news at times other than when I was playing cards helped me to gain acceptance by the other students and, in general, move more deeply into the UPJ White student community. After one discussion of current events, a highly sought after, sexually attractive, high achieving White girl said to me, "Jack, I've been telling my parents about you."

Surprised and eager to interact with her, I responded quickly with, "Oh, really? Elaine, what have you been telling them?" Seemingly with pride, she gushed, "That you and George are probably the two best Bridge players at school, that you just learned to play, and that you're so good they should play you."

Disappointed by not receiving an invitation to play her and one of her female friends as well as curious about why she wanted us to play her parents, I inquired, "But why your parents?"

Elaine explained, "They have tournament experience and it would be just so cool if you were able to whip their pants off!"

Taking what was offered, I accepted the invitation and assured her that George would do the same. That next weekend, George used his parents' car to drive us to Elaine's beautiful home in an all-White, upper class neighborhood. Elaine's mother met us at the door, and said, "I'm Mary, Elaine's mother. It's so wonderful that 'you boys' are attending UPJ." We followed her to a cherry wood paneled game room where Elaine invited us to try a few of the finger sandwiches on a silver platter. Her father, Bob, joined us about ten minutes later and handed each of us a beer.

Never before had I sat in leather card table chairs at an unblemished felt covered table. I gawked at the large television, ping pong table, lush carpet, oil painting of Mickey Mantle, and other lavish furnishings in the game room. My attention was also drawn to Elaine's tanned legs extending from her UPJ blue and gold shorts, the bright red lipstick that seemed to enlarge her normally thin lips, and her increasingly flushed cheeks as she drank beers at a pace that would have rendered me drunk. Lust for her and admiration of her family's furnishings swirled through my mind, causing my Bridge playing to suffer through the first several games.

George's critical comments regarding my play caused me to regroup. Subsequently, we won three games in a row. However, I was not bothered that her parents edged out a victory in the final match. When they left the room to make coffee and get snacks, George began a conversation with Elaine. I walked around looking closely at the room's furnishing and vicariously enjoyed the good life. It was so gratifying to have been invited to this lavish suburban home, to have played cards with Elaine's liberal parents who insisted that we call them by their first names, and to have done something in such a home other than domestic work which I occasionally did with my mother to help pay college expenses.

My self-esteem received another artificial boost after I overheard the following kitchen conversation. "Mary, those two kids are amazing! Wait until our friends see what we have discovered. Let's invite them to the Club the next time we play." A little reticent, Mary, asked, "Bob, don't you think some of our friends will object?" It seemed so supportive when he answered, "Maybe Paul and Madeline will. You know how they are at times, but they'll get over it when they see these two colored kids play." Mary added, "Okay, let's invite them. They are just super when it comes to their bidding and playing. I've never seen anything like it. They seem to come by it naturally. They'll probably be a hit with most of our friends."

When Elaine's father invited us to his club, I was so mesmerized that it never occurred to me that anyone could have associated our "amazing" Bridge play with the comical incongruity of two "monkeys" merely being able to play Bridge, much less play at the level that we had reached. No, I was on the fast track to true integration into the community of good, educated, and wealthy White people.

I was ceasing to be an ordinary Black from the projects, the stereotypical over-sexed male who impregnated women but never functioned fully as a father. I was not the ruffian whose primary delicacy was warm watermelon after plucking it off the vine and bursting it open on a nearby rock. Instead of becoming the beast of burden good for nothing but hard labor, Jack Daniel was transitioning into a fine gentleman who could enjoy delicate finger sandwiches and engage in polite conversation about current events.

I had no hint of the possibility that George and I had been permitted to enter the "Big House" to perform very limited entertaining roles. My anxious-to-be-accepted self could not imagine little Black idiot savants serving as the added attraction at a racially segregated country club and/or the heretofore all-White UPJ student body. Instead, I persisted in believing that I was reaping the benefits of learning games that demanded higher cognitive performance than the more primitive Black games of chance. There would be no more low life dice playing in alleys and heavy-drinking at Bid Whist public housing rent parties. Mine would be the good life modeled by Elaine's parents. Constant complainers about the "White man" could better themselves too if they were willing to follow my lead.

I might have succeeded in rejecting what I thought to be my ugly Black past and become the quintessential "Oreo" often mocked in my community, but for the fact that I was only permitted to hang around the fringes of the UPJ student culture, to merely peep through the window of Bridge and view a tiny bit of the world inhabited by upwardly mobile White youth.

Painful memories of my hopeless efforts to assimilate came rushing back when, as an adult, I examined my UPJ cultural assimilation experiences through the lens of the following excerpt from Black Skin, White Masks' third chapter, "The Man of Color and the White Woman."

> *Out of the blackest part of my soul, across the zebra striping of my mind, surges, this desire to be suddenly "white." ... who but a white woman can do this for me? By loving me she proves that I am worthy of white love. I am loved like a white man. I am a white man. Her love takes me onto the noble road that leads to total realization...*

A rather ordinary looking White female, Noreen, was my favorite Bridge partner when George was absent. She was also the woman I briefly hoped would salvage my soiled soul and put me on a path toward "total realization." Seeking to know her not only as a card player but also in the Biblical sense, I began to have occasional bag lunches with her followed by long walks around campus. Discussions of campus life gave way to complaints about her parents, and, after a few weeks, we talked about ways to resolve racial difficulties. We agreed that the world would be much better if people took time to understand each other as we were doing. Love appeared to be on the way when one of her goodbyes was accompanied by a soft kiss on my cheek and the exclamation, "Jack, I just love being with you! You make me feel so relaxed!"

Descent from my euphoric mountain began a few days afterwards when I hesitantly told George, "Uh, George, I, uh, need to talk with you about something." With a very concerned look on his face, he asked, "What's up man? Did somebody just kick your butt or something?" I answered, "Well, in a way, something is kicking my butt. You know I've been spending a lot of time with Noreen, and we've really started getting close and ..." George interrupted with laughter and asked, "Close? What the hell is close?" Meekly, I answered, "I'm thinking Noreen could be someone I'd marry."

George asked in a loud and disgusting voice, "Nigger, are you crazy?" With the sense of shame associated with a racial sell out, I lied, "No, man, I was just joking." George added, "I sure hope you were" and we went our separate ways.

Privately, I thought my closest friend was jealous of the fact that I was loved by a White woman who just might accept my marriage proposal, that he had yet to find a way out of the hell that engulfed members of our community. A week later, I was disabused of that fantasy when Noreen rushed up to me and blurted out, "Jack, I just got engaged!" Dumfounded, I said nothing until she asked, "Why aren't you happy for me?" I made the lame reply, "I'm just so happy for you that I don't know what to say."

Noreen's inadvertent clarification of our relationship paled in comparison to the ways other White students made "my place" clear to me and I adjusted to their stereotypical definitions of "my place" on campus. For example, none of my community friends viewed me as a good dancer. With them, I stuck primarily to "slow dragging" or "grinding" on songs such as "One Summer Night" and "For Your Precious Love." Driven to assimilate at UPJ, I quickly learned the White students' spastic dance steps, eagerly combined them with my poor sense of rhythm, and became part of their entertainment.

At one campus party, someone played "A Whole Lot of Shaking Going On," and a guy yelled, "Come on, Jack! Show us your stuff! Go man, go!" Anxious to please, I complied with gyrations that I didn't know I could perform, moves that would have brought hysterical laughter back in my community. As I danced my jig, I might as well have added a refrain from those old movies in which the eye-popping Black man shouted, "Feets, do yo stuff!"

Later that evening, I received an additional reality check. Hearing one of my favorite songs, "Save the Last Dance for Me," I began a slow suggestive Cha Cha with a much sought-after White girl wearing a very tight skirt. We had danced less than thirty seconds before some of the guys whistled, made cat calls, and taunted in other ways. She became so embarrassed that she quit dancing before the song was half over. I tried to tell myself that they were jealous of my dance steps, but the truth was confirmed a few minutes later when I started to slow dance with another White girl.

One guy stumbled into me, knocking me almost off my feet. He blamed his alcohol consumption, but his laughter and that of his buddies contradicted him. I kept dancing and someone else bumped the record player, causing the record to scratch terribly and the song to end. While fixing the record player, another guy asked me to tell a joke. As polite young White men, only a few of them ever told dirty jokes in mixed gender venues where I was allowed to participate. Motivated by my huge desire for acceptance, I told at least one sexually explicit joke per party. By doing so, I confirmed the fact that I too was a joke, someone not to taken seriously, socially or in the classroom.

Acquiring a college education necessarily includes learning new ideas, beliefs and values, but the price need not include acting like a buffoon and rejecting one's cultural origins. Unfortunately, like most other historically White schools at the time, UPJ had no Black Studies courses; there were no Black faculty, staff, or guest speakers; we never had a campus observation of Black History month; and, in sum, the campus never did anything that might have provided me with cultural stability.

On the contrary, the UPJ history curriculum was primarily a two-course sequence on the History of Western Civilization. As future leaders, UPJ students should not have had their heads buried in the sands of western civilization while, for example, China along with countries from the Middle East and Africa were becoming increasingly important to our economy. UPJ's narrow cultural and intellectual foci penalized all of its students by not preparing them to live in an increasingly variegated American society and to function as citizens of the world. For my part, I remained intellectually and culturally adrift, notwithstanding my efforts to bridge the student cultural chasm I experienced at UPJ.

CHAPTER FOUR:

The Quintessential First-Generation College Student

...The worthy fruit of academic culture is an open mind, trained to careful thinking, instructed in the methods of philosophic investigation, acquainted in a general way with the accumulated thought of past genera-tions, and penetrated with humility. It is thus that the university in our day serves Christ and the church... Charles W. Eliot in his inaugural address as President of Harvard, 1869

Notwithstanding the still celebrated statements of Charles E. Eliot, to this day the aims of a liberal arts education is an evolving matter, often debated by senior academicians. The vast majority of students begin their college careers in "liberal arts" programs but with no significant understanding of "liberal arts." Even students who are academically highly qualified and whose parents were college graduates do not adequately comprehend the aims of a liberal arts education. For example, they do not understand the reasons why institutions have "distribution of studies" requirements that mandate specific levels of courses in math, science, English and foreign languages. They do not understand fully the purposes of "majors" and "minors."

Without comprehensive programs that introduce first-year students to the campus, the curriculum and the community, many academic pitfalls await undergraduates. As was the case for me, the dangers are even greater for first-generation college students whose parents did not graduate from college and did not have the background experiences to help their children negotiate their first year in college.

In my case, not only was "liberal arts" not a part of my vocabulary, but it was also the case that I had reduced a "college education" to a matter of earning credits and grades. Engulfed in my ignorance, I experienced several incidents that almost caused me to cease my pursuit of my baccalaureate degree. In addition, my first college semester was disastrous because my very low academic self-esteem caused me to place a higher premium on achieving social recognition from White students rather than succeeding academically. Partying, competing in intramural basketball, playing cards, and participating in other social activities became normative for me, although always lurking in the back of my mind was my pending academic doom.

Added to my counterproductive behavior was the fact that I was clueless when it came to knowing the nature of effective study skills, help was never offered, and I never sought help from my professors who, for the most part, seemed to simply tolerate my presence. Like many eighteen-year-old first generation college students, I also saw no meaningful connections between grades, required courses, majors, degrees, careers, and eventual life styles.

Classes with labs posed a special problem because I was usually one of the last to obtain a lab partner. Typically, faculty members did not assign students to serve as lab partners. However, in one instance, the professor added me to a team of what I perceived to be nerds who cared more about biology than my presence. These guys dressed sloppily, seemed to lack interest in girls, and showed no concern with me as a lab partner. That lab report led to my one "A" grade among the many "C" or lower grades I received for other lab assignments.

I had no success in gaining access to the students' academic support systems, though admittedly I infrequently tried to do so. An invitation to join a study group never came my way, and there was never room for another person the few times I inquired about joining a group. First-year study groups had solidified by the time I received a "D" on the Biology mid-term exam and overheard some of their members discussing the ways their study groups had helped them earn high grades.

Educators know that successfully integrating first-year students into the campus community is a key factor related to student retention. Not only did UPJ not offer such support, it was also the case that it was late during my first semester that I began to realize that social networks, intimate relations, and other forms of interpersonal bonding grew out of and contributed to the study group affiliations. It didn't take long for me to learn I was not the type of "bird" the "flocks" craved. Understandably, people preferred academically high achieving students, but there were instances in which lower performers were pursued, particularly if they added some form of social prestige to the group.

Although some students eagerly sought me out to play Bridge and would adjust their out-of-class schedules to fit mine, these same students made no adjustments to their study group times and places to accommodate me in their study circles. They saw me as a barren academic field and saw no reason to try and cultivate the soil of my mind.

I remained on the periphery of other aspects of UPJ's self-help student culture. Students often swapped used textbooks, but George and I were primarily limited to exchanging books with each other. It took a truly a rare book with absolutely no other buyer for the owner to bring it to my attention. Seeking to save money by sharing a single copy of books for courses during the second term, George and I enrolled in three of the same courses, but between the two of us, we still did not have enough money to purchase all of the required books. We sometimes made use of the library's copies of required texts.

I eventually resorted to my "when effort fails, sympathy prevails" strategy which functioned best with my Spanish professor who, for reasons unknown to me, cared deeply about my succeeding at UPJ. Knowing that I could not perform well enough to earn a "C," I scheduled a meeting with her. For approximately a half hour before the meeting, I rehearsed lines which became part of the following conversation that unquestionably saved my floundering semester.

I began by blurting out, "Mi madre es pobre. Mi padre es pobre. Mi heramano es pobre y espanol es muy dificil por me. Me gusta tu professor, pero espanol es muy dificil por me."

Not moved by my use of Spanish, my professor asked, "Well, Jack, how much do you study?"

Lying, I answered, "Muchas horas per dia, pero, no lo comprendo."

Looking deeply concerned and in a passionate voice, she said, "It is so important that you succeed at UPJ. Your success will mean a lot in terms of others like you coming here. I probably should not do this, but if you come to class every day, sit in the front row, and hand in all written assignments, you should be able to receive a 'C.'"

"Muchas gracias, professor," I stated in my best Spanish articulation. She smiled and said, "De nada."

It might well have been nothing for the Spanish professor to reward my minimally compliant behavior with a "C," but it was literally short-term academic survival for me and, still worse, her "social pass" did nothing to help end my counterproductive academic mindset. I ended the term knowing little more than basic Spanish idiomatic expressions as well as rudimentary grammar and syntax. However, her gift grade plus that of other professors provided me with the cumulative grade point average I needed to return for a second term.

My psychology professor had taken to enlivening his class by often calling on me when no other student responded to his probing questions. My sometimes obviously wrong answers were often followed by laughter, much like what transpired when I was in grade school and purposely acted stupid in the lowest performing Yellow Bird group. Knowing that I received "C" grades or less on my psychology exams and papers, I assumed that the final "B" grade was a reward for being my professor's foil. However, I unwittingly benefitted from his questioning as it had caused me to pay closer attention in class, aroused my interest in the course content, and, in retrospect, contributed to my decision to major in Psychology.

I didn't care how the psychology grade was derived. My primary concern was obtaining that fate determining "C" average, and I desperately needed at least a "B" in Psychology to offset the "D" I was sure to receive in Biology. The latter grade came in consequence of a grade of "F" given by my Biology lab instructor after he discovered that I was the one who scratched my teeth with a toothpick, wiped the substance in one of his Petri jars, and contaminated one of his cultures.

I obtained a mystery "C," probably a third gift, in English. Throughout the term, my papers came back covered with negative comments from the professor. Most of the grades were "D" or "C." I tried to convince myself that I had done well on the final paper for the course, a paper that I never bothered to retrieve. However, my English teacher knew how poorly I wrote and, given the importance of basic writing skills, his "C" left me academically crippled. Absent a reason to change, I remained mired in the muck of my "get over," self-destructive mentality of putting forth the least effort to obtain the minimum academic outcomes.

I continued on my minimal effort path until the summer after my second semester. UPJ had begun to experiment with a "trimester" system whereby high achieving and financially able students could take a full load of courses during the summer. By doing so, one could graduate in two and two-thirds chronological years. I had been unable to acquire a summer job in Johnstown and, given my skimpy grade point average, my oldest brother, Russell, paid my third term tuition hoping that I would improve academically. Before the semester began, he also gave me money to purchase my books. Bored while waiting for the term to start, I read a couple of chapters in several of them. Even with that head start, I was headed for disaster until, my ignorance created an opportunity for me.

While sitting in the student lounge waiting for Bridge players on the second day of third-term classes, I noted three of UPJ's best students discussing a plan for maintaining their "A" averages. I got up to get a drink from the water fountain near them and used that as an opportunity to sit closer to them. Essentially, I overheard the following: First, each person read the appropriate book chapters in advance of the classes when the professor discussed the material. During their initial readings, they agreed to use green ink to highlight anything they thought to be important. Subsequently, they carried their books to class and each used a yellow marker to highlight anything the professor emphasized but they had not previously highlighted in green. If the professor mentioned a green highlight, then they would put a red check mark in the margins. Several days before a test, among other things within their study group, they discussed the course content related to their color markings. Completely ignorant of effective learning skills, I literally thought the students were cheating!

The students' effective learning approach collided with how I had been raised. The Bible, Sunday School books, a few Masonic and Eastern Star texts, and the dictionary made up the library in my home. Books, especially the Bible being the word of God, were precious, and to write in a book was nearly a sin. However, for academic survival purposes, I decided to use the color coding system and shed yet another part of my cultural beliefs. By adopting more "White" ways, not only might I give my cumulative average a boost, I might also have more time to play Bridge in the fall when most of the good players returned.

Doing required reading in advance of class was quite a dramatic change for me, given that I could not recall having ever done all required readings for a class. Indeed, until that summer at UPJ, I had never read a book in its entirety but had come close to completing a ruffled copy of <u>Memoirs of a Woman of Pleasure</u> that had been circulated secretly among some guys in high school. Another new experience was being very attentive in class in order to check my green markings against the content of the lectures.

The above process immediately yielded dividends when the professors' lectures led me to place red marks by so many of my green marks. I became ecstatic when I received an "A" on my first exam and, for the first time, formal learning became fun. Using the process led to a 3.6 grade point average for that term. The very next semester, however, my enthusiasm for learning was deflated by three key events, some of which might have been avoided had UPJ provided all students with things such as career counselling and internships. Consider, for example, what transpired when I was an Air Force ROTC cadet.

After a several weeks of hazing, I became a member of the Pershing Rifles ROTC drill team. This was something in which I excelled. Everyone knew I was one of the very best at trick drill and was a key to the team advancing to the final rounds of the regional ROTC competition. Never having received career counselling related to a successful career as a military officer, I thought my Pershing Rifle success made me as important to the Air Force ROTC as the star quarterback was to our high school football team. However, my success in these areas did not carry over to the classroom where, not having sufficiently read and studied the written material, I struggled to earn "C+" grades on exams but received a final "B" grade. Still, I thought I was the logical choice for becoming the new Cadet Commander.

On the September morning of the big announcement, I was among the first to check the ROTC bulletin board. In big bold blue letters, there appeared the name of another cadet. Naively, I thought he was a real joke with not one iota of the qualities associated with the authoritative command voice I deemed important for the new Cadet Commander. Full of anger, I decided to immediately meet with the ROTC Professor of Military Science.

After I knocked, was invited in, saluted, and stood before him, the ROTC Professor asked, "Cadet Daniel, is there an urgent matter? I don't have you scheduled for an appointment."

Defiantly, I looked him in his eyes, snapped, "Sir, I came to resign, sir!"

Perplexed, the Professor ordered, "At ease."

Remaining stiff, I replied, "Sir, there's no way I can take orders from the new Cadet Commander, a less qualified White guy!"

In a raised voice, the Professor demanded, "Hold on! Hold on! You're putting race where it doesn't belong. You have a seat and listen to me young man!"

I listened as the professor explained that race had nothing to do with his selection of the Cadet Commander, and I said nothing in response to his noting that I had never earned an "A" grade on an ROTC class assignment. Then he cautioned me, "Your grades and attitude are in need of serious work, if you aspire to a leadership role. You're not going to get very far in life if, because of race, you can't take orders from a highly qualified person. I suggest that you leave now and reconsider what you said to me. You're dismissed!"

I stood, saluted, spun sharply around, and marched out of his office. For me, it was a race-based decision and that was that. Knowing nothing about real war, I sincerely believed that grit not good grades would carry the day on a battlefield. The injustice seemed so clear to me that, the very next morning, I turned in my uniform, dropped my ROTC class, and added a Psychology class. Why bother holding fast to a dream racism made unattainable?

Without the prospect of serving as an Air Force officer and, again having received no career counseling or related academic advising, I naively gave thought to becoming a psychologist. I had received three "B" or better grades in psychology courses, the material was of increasing interest, and I often discussed concepts with friends and relatives back home. I was especially intrigued by the symbolic interpretation of dreams, given the many times I had heard the biblical stories involving the dream interpreter, Joseph. In addition, Mama and many other family members often translated their dreams into what number to play in the illegal daily lottery. Now, with the most rudimentary knowledge, I began to enjoy interpreting people's dreams and general behavior.

After several lengthy discussions, I convinced one hometown guy that he was paranoid and needed to quit being so suspicious of everyone. A young overweight lady drank excessively and, after discussing the nature of the depression I deemed to be associated with her weight and limited finances, I persuaded her to give up the bottle and walk several mornings with me. These successful outcomes and my increasingly solicited and accepted "love relationship advice" led to my friends and adults calling me "the shrink." Shortly, I too began to think of myself as "the shrink," a budding psychologist.

About a month after I enthusiastically declared a Psychology major, my academic confidence was wrecked by remarks from an English professor. I had enrolled in her class because I heard she used a psychological approach to literary criticism, and I was very excited when she asked me to come to her office to discuss the last paper I had submitted. Once seated in her office, she casually began with, "I'm glad you came. How are you doing in your other classes?"

Not knowing where she was headed, I simply replied, "Okay. I know that I'll end up with more than a 3.0 average this term."

She smiled a bit and added, "Well, you know, test grades aren't everything there is to learning. Having excellent writing skills is quite important too. You do well on my tests, but your writing needs considerable improvement. Here, take a look at my comments on your last paper."

On just about every page, there were red ink comments. Many misspelled words were circled. Commas had been inserted, new paragraphs were suggested, references were made to inconsistent verb tenses, and some items simply had a deletion line drawn through them. The number of comments was shocking; neither of us said another word for what seemed several minutes. I turned the pages ever so slowly, wondering if the next page would have even more critical comments. Embarrassed both by the sea of red and my miscalculation regarding the purpose of the meeting, I continued to stare at the pages.

Breaking the silence, my professor said sincerely, "I'm very concerned with basic things such as your grammatical constructions. Aren't you a Psychology major?" I answered, "Yes, but what's that got to do with my writing?" Then she advised, "You will never get into or succeed in graduate school with that kind of writing." Trying to be nice, but seeking to end an uncomfortable discussion, I politely informed her, "I'm not going to graduate school. I'm going straight into practice when I finish my degree." She blushed, smiled, composed herself, and asked, "You're going to do what?"

Confidently, I repeated my plans and added, "Actually, I have a small practice now. My friend George and I practice many Saturday nights at the Coke Plant Club in Conemaugh. George is Sociology major and, when we work together, we complement each other. He knows about groups. I know about individuals. Although we are not old enough to get into the Coke Plant Club, my uncles and a few other men get us past the entrance. We usually go on Saturday nights when a lot of single female parents and men without jobs are there.

Most of the women are much older than we are, but they love talking to us. We listen and give them free advice. Well, it's not exactly free because they buy us drinks and sometimes they give us hugs, kisses, and a slow dance or two. Women can hardly wait to talk with us. As soon as I walk through the door, someone shouts, 'The young doctor is in! Boy, come over here and work on my head!'"

After ending the account of my burgeoning clinical practice, my professor asked, "Do you realize that what you are doing might be illegal?" I said, "No, we don't get paid. Like I said, just a few drinks and so forth." Quite concerned, she asked, "Do you know the differences between a psychologist and a psychiatrist?" Believing that I had not made my professional goal clear to her, I answered, "No, but why do I need to know about a psychiatrist when I am becoming a psychologist? With her face displaying considerable amazement, she asked, "Do you even know what degree you need to be a licensed psychologist?" Perplexed, I asked, "What do you mean by licensed, other than my bachelor's degree?" Seemingly horrified, she asked, "Who has been advising you?"

Still not getting it, I told her, "I sign up for classes with whichever advisor is available." She pressed further with, "Yes, but in addition to signing up for classes, who advised you regarding which courses to take for your distribution of studies, your major, and your career goals? Have you ever discussed your career goals with an academic advisor?" I answered, "No. When I first started, my advisor just gave me some basic courses and told me that I needed a 'C' average. He signed me up for a psychology class and several other basic courses. The second term, I just took another Psychology class because I received a "B" in the first." I became more interested in psychology after I quit ROTC."

Then came her astonishing revelation, "Jack, you need a doctorate to become a psychologist. Medical doctors specialize in psychiatry." Bewildered, I asked, "What, a doctor's degree to become a psychologist?" and she answered, "Yes, you would have to go to graduate school and, my concern is that you will never succeed in graduate school because of your poor writing."

My embarrassment descended to dismay as my second career interest seemed to be quickly vanishing. Having heard from my parents that a four-year college education was worth so much in terms of improving my life and, never investigating further on my own, I had only thought in terms of accumulating 120 credits with at least a "C" average and a major in psychology --nothing more, nothing less.

Admissions criteria aside, my woefully inadequate financial circumstances made paying for graduate study seem like an impossible dream. Now, since I was neither becoming an Air Force officer nor a psychologist, I was prepared to end my relationship with UPJ. It seemed as though a very cruel trick had been played on me. When I was told about the great chance being given to me, the only explicit academic expectation was that I maintain passing grades for two terms. Now, my earned honor grades would not be sufficient for becoming a psychologist because of my writing problems. My literature professor offered me no solution other than, "pay closer attention to your writing" and, very honestly, I did not know how to do that.

Amidst this confusion came the even more devastating feedback that there was something wrong with my speaking. I had enrolled in the course, "Speech in a Free Society." For one of my speaking assignments, I chose "Race in America." In preparation, for the first time in my life, I read an entire book written by an African American, Strides Toward Freedom, by Martin Luther King Jr. I began and ended my speech with, "We Shall Overcome." One of my vivid illustrations consisted of detailing life in segregated, roach infested, overcrowded, public housing at a poverty level that led to realities such as "ketchup sandwiches," "mustard sandwiches," and some of those sandwiches plus water constituting the one and only meal for the day.

When a few students laughed, I regretted having exaggerated about the sandwiches. They developed a more serious mood, however, when I quoted from Thoreau's writing on civil disobedience as well as the works of Mahatma Gandhi and Martin Luther King Jr. After I ended, students applauded for the first and only time following any student's speech during the semester. The teacher gave me an "A," although he requested that I meet with him.

After the other students had left the room, my Speech Professor said, "I'll have to make this quick. Your content was excellent, but you had quite a few double negatives throughout your remarks. Also, you keep saying "dis" for "this" and "goin" and "comin" for "going" and "coming." For example, you said, "Dere's 'goin' to be a time when all people, not 'jes' White people will be free." Sometimes you said 'gonna' instead of 'going' and that's just not the way college educated people talk."

His comments left me feeling quite ambivalent. I didn't know if he was right, if there were some standard rules I had violated, or if it was just a matter of his trying to get me to talk in what I perceived to be a White, socially acceptable fashion. Since I continued to receive more "A" grades from this professor, I decided to ignore his comments despite the fact that he made comments about my articulation after each subsequent speech.

It seemed as if there was no end to what I would have to do to succeed in college. Having been deemed unable to write or speak well and, being neither willing to invest in the improvement of my writing nor change my articulation patterns, I lost interest in using the color-coding system to earn high grades. I reasoned that even if I earned a 4.0, then some White person would still find something wrong with me.

Langston Hughes' "Hold Fast to Dreams" describes well the tremendous disappointment I initially experienced with my first two years of higher education. With my dreams dashed, I was in the state of mind Hughes described as a "...a barren field filled with snow." I was the "broken-winged bird" he described as unable to fly. Having internalized my inability to fly, I wondered why I should try. I had no answer to that question other than the fear of facing my parents' tremendous disappointment if I failed to earn a baccalaureate degree. Once again, therefore, I set forth on a self-fulfilling course of low academic expectations, doing just enough to get a diploma and make my parents happy.

With financial help from my brother Russell, parents, and loans, I decided to take a second summer semester of courses which would enable me to graduate in two and two-third years and then get on with my life. Right after graduation, I planned to cram for a civil service examination and get a job based on my test score. Russell had told me about his many Black Philadelphia friends who graduated from college, but worked in the Post Office and earned more than teachers. At the time, I did not realize that civil service was the upward mobility route taken by many Black college graduates when racism prevented them from taking jobs more relevant to their formal education. Civil service was simply the vague path I sought to embrace at a time when I was in great need of the personal, academic and career counseling I did not receive at UPJ.

As valuable as career counseling is for academically well-prepared students, it is an even more critical component of any program designed for disadvantaged students. And, to the extent that they possess the counter productive baggage I carried to UPJ, such counseling should be mandatory.

When less fortunate individuals are immersed in a community of low expectations and achievement, it is essential that they receive exposure to career opportunities and role models to help them believe in a world of possibilities, not one constrained by limitations. They cannot be left to their own devices as I was, hoping for passing grades from sympathetic professors as opposed to believing in their ability to achieve at the highest levels if they put forth an equally high effort.

CHAPTER FIVE:

Entry into a Segregated Campus Community

As a freshman, I knew UPJ did not offer a baccalaureate degree and I had to transfer to the Pittsburgh campus for degree completion. However, like the fabled grasshopper, I fiddled throughout most of my last summer at UPJ while other transferring students made plans for the coming semester. Reality seized me when I overheard a student excitedly telling his friend how fortunate he was to have found a Pittsburgh apartment during the Fourth of July break.

I became quite worried when, after inquiring about the cost for a Pittsburgh apartment, the guy indicated he was fortunate to be paying only $55 per month by sharing an apartment with two other UPJ students. I had neither friends with whom I might share an apartment in Pittsburgh nor more than $55 a month for an apartment by myself. Moreover, unlike the established network that White transfer students had established, I lacked information regarding how to find an affordable place to stay near the University in a racially segregated Pittsburgh.

Panic set in after I contacted the Pittsburgh campus' housing office and learned that names were no longer being added to the student housing waiting list. Dismayed by the outcomes of my foolishness, I feverishly spent the next several days completing job applications. My intent was to get a job in September, save as much as I could, make a timely application for student housing, and transfer to Pittsburgh in January. My fate took a positive turn after I discussed my housing problem with Martha, a Johnstown friend who was currently living in Pittsburgh.

Martha put me in contact with Ms. Marjorie Butler, a Black adult doctoral student, who owned a four-bedroom home located in the predominantly Black Hill District about a fifteen-minute walk from the Pittsburgh campus. Ms. Butler had one son living with her, rented rooms to Pitt students, and had a vacancy. After she interviewed me by telephone, Ms. Butler offered me a small bedroom plus the general use of the common areas of her home. She gave me two weeks to send her $40 for the first month's rent to secure the room. As had been the case several times when I was desperate to meet a college expense, my brother Russell came through for me and forwarded the check to Ms. Butler.

On the Saturday before the start of my senior year, my friend George drove me to Pittsburgh where we stayed at the home of his relatives. After we arrived, we went to meet Ms. Butler and drop off a footlocker containing all of my possessions. She enthusiastically greeted us, asked about our academic interests, and then mentioned nearby Black churches, barbershops, and other places she thought might be of interest to us. Then she suggested that we might explore the campus.

Believing it to be the residence hall for Pitt's athletes, the first building that we went to was the Athletic Club located directly across the street from Pitt's main building, the Cathedral of Learning. We hadn't gotten to the middle of the lobby before a man approached us and declared, "You two are in the wrong place. This is a private club." He then proceeded to escort us out of the building. Standing outside and feeling stupid, we decided to go to the bookstore and check the prices of my required texts.

We hadn't browsed for more than fifteen minutes before I noticed a student wearing a purple and gold Omega Psi Phi fraternity shirt. I had heard of this Black fraternity but had never met a member. Curious, I told George to check out the guy's shirt and suggested that we go meet him. We walked over, exchanged greetings, and informed him that I was coming to Pittsburgh to complete my degree and that George would be coming the next year. He expressed how happy he was to meet us because there were so few Blacks on campus and then invited us to his fraternity's party later that night. We eagerly accepted the invitation.

We arrived around 9:30 p.m. and the fraternity brother's father directed us to the basement which was full of laughter and lit up in the classic "blue lights in the basement" fashion. There were about twenty students present. Most of the female students were members of the Delta Sigma Theta sorority. George, I, and two other guys were the only non-fraternity members. After more than an hour of meeting people, dancing, and drinking heavily spiked punch, I heard the very familiar Bid Whist exclamations of "Three," "Four special," and "Four no trump," followed by a boisterous "Hell no! I'm taking that out! Five special!"

George and I immediately went to the adjacent room, and I declared, "If you all are not afraid, we've got the next seats!" Accepting the challenge, one member of the winning team said, "Okay, we'll soon need some new turkeys. We'll probably beat you in two hands, if we don't run a Boston on the first one." When we finally got a chance to play, we soundly defeated three teams before we lost. Not wanting to hear the winners' trash talking nor willing to wait for a rematch, I quickly left the game room to check out various females who appeared unattached.

After two or three failed attempts to make a connection, Colette, a gorgeous, well developed, chocolate-to-the-bone, upper class student slowed danced with me, and I dropped some lines about wanting to meet people, being anxious to do well academically, and desiring to join study groups. The faked academic emphasis seemed to do the trick because Colette gave me her telephone number as well as directions to the on-campus fast food restaurant called the Tuck Shop where she agreed to meet me on the first day of classes and introduce me to other academically serious students.

Like so many other situations on historically White campuses, absent a private space to gather, the least desirable area of the Tuck Shop became the meeting place for Black students. Long ago when only Whites attended Pitt, various White student organizations had claimed the Tuck Shop booths that were located nearest the food lines, could comfortably accommodate larger numbers of students, and had newer furniture as well as brighter lighting. Black Greek organizations posted messages on a bulletin board and, at noon, met pledges in their small, remote, dingy corner which was often over heated during the spring and summer, had no windows, and served as the work station for the janitors to store equipment, empty garbage, and dump dirty water after scrubbing the floors.

Hanging out in the Tuck Shop was my entry into the racially segregated Pittsburgh campus student community. There were a few former UPJ White students on campus, but we made no effort to contact each other. Instead, we quickly learned our racial places and chose to stay in them. For example, at on-campus parties, Blacks danced in one small corner of the ballroom while White students occupied the majority of the floor space. At football games, Blacks sat near the end zone. Whites occupied the primary student section. Similarly, Black and White students sat in their respective sections of the student cafeterias.

In 1962, only a handful of Black students lived in the residence halls and the primary daytime "cafeteria" was the Tuck Shop. Hence, on the first day of classes for my senior year, I decided to make what I believed to be an early 11 a.m. arrival in the Tuck Shop. To my great surprise, before I rounded the last corner, I could hear loud talking and raucous laughter coming from that section. Several Bid Whist games were in progress and Colette sat at one table. When her card partner had to leave, she invited me to take his place. Captured by the deep cleavage displayed by her tight white V-necked blouse as well as her card playing skills, I played until shortly before our two o'clock classes. As I left, an onlooker said, "Uh, oh, another one of these people majoring in Bid Whist. He'll be flunking out by the end of the term." Everyone laughed but, by the end of the term, more than a few students experienced serious academic difficulties as a result of excessively playing Bid Whist.

Things never materialized beyond friendship with Colette, but one noon I got mesmerized by a tall, brown-eyed, dark-skinned, pledge of the Black sorority Alpha Kappa Alpha. Like a bee uncontrollably drawn to the brightest flower, my eyes scanned the skinny waist that connected her breasts and the type of butt that caused us guys to say, "Baby got back." Completely taken, I started mumbling to myself a memorable line from the great comedian, Red Foxx, i.e., "the Lord is my shepherd and I see what I want." As soon as she entered the food line, I dashed over to her and quickly said, "I'm Jack Daniel, new from Johnstown, and I'm trying to meet people. What's your name?"

A bit reticent, she responded, "Jerri Colley, and I see you like to play cards. When do you study?"

I lied stating, "Oh, I study long hours at night." Then, in pursuit of my primary agenda, I quickly asked, "Mind if I buy you a drink?"

"That's okay; I have to get some chips for my big sister. So, what's your major?"

As we were approaching the cashier, I hurriedly responded, "Psychology, and what's yours?"

"Political Science and Spanish," she said in a matter of fact tone.

Impressed, I responded, "Wow, a double major! I know your sorority sister is waiting for you to get back. How about giving me your room number and perhaps we can talk more about our majors."

The partial frown on her face suggested that I was being more than presumptuous, but something made her change her mind as she quickly whispered, "420 Holland Hall." Later that day, I learned from one of her pledge sisters that Jerri was from Sacramento California, had entered Pitt when she was only 17 years-old, and was an academically serious sophomore. The latter point provided the basis of a scheme for connecting with her.

My Sociology class happened to be focusing on the role of individual leaders and group memberships in shaping one's beliefs and behavior. Consequently, with my first interviewee being Jerri, I decided to do a research project during which I ascertained the most influential Black student groups and individuals on campus. Surely my student research would impress her and, if it didn't, then the interview process might yield still other significant females with whom I might pursue romantic goals.

We met in a student lounge and, after the interview was completed, Jerri smiled and said, "You're very smart. This is the most interesting piece of work I've seen a student do for a paper. So, why do you spend so much time playing cards and hanging out with those other 'Whistologists' in the Tuck Shop?"

Keeping up the initial lie I had told her, I explained, "Well, I study so much at home all hours of the night that I need to relax while on campus. If we could spend more time like this evening, I'd give up playing cards. What do you do to relax?"

When she told me that she loved to bowl, I excitedly said, "Oh, wow! I worked in a bowling alley. I got pretty good at bowling, even bowled in a junior league. You've got to let me take you bowling."

Seeming to be stalling a bit, Jerri stated, "Well, I've got two big exams coming up and I'm not sure of my big sisters' plans. What day do you have in mind?" "This Saturday evening," I offered. To my surprise she agreed and asked me to drop by her dorm around 7 p.m. I made the reservations and thus began a series of bowling dates. Things progressed rapidly and, for Thanksgiving, I gave her my high school graduation ring. By the end of the term, we were a serious couple.

Interestingly, both on the UPJ and the Pittsburgh campus it was a culturally loaded card game that provided me with entry into segregated campus communities. I used Bridge in an effort to break into the UPJ White community, Bid Whist to come back home to my Black community. Given the blatant racism that has erupted since the election of POTUS 45, it seems that for the foreseeable future racially separated student communities will persist.

Segregated campus life has persisted, notwithstanding the many present day efforts associated with diversity and inclusion. An excellent testament to the enduring nature of racism on historically White campuses is the fact that Why Are All The Black Kids Sitting Together in the Cafeteria was first published in 1977, was revised in 2003, and continues to be a text professors use in social science classes.

A first-year, living-learning seminar for a small group of students will, at best, be a bandage for those enrolled given that White students are increasingly less reticent to hold "Cinco de Drinko" parties; pose in blackface; stage "shock your mom" parties at which time some White students wear cornrows and bandanas; and serve watermelon at a Martin Luther King Jr. holiday party. Change of such deep-rooted racism might have to await the time when people of color constitute the vast majority of American citizens, including students on the campuses of historically White institutions, and someone writes a text, "Why are all the White Students Sitting Together in the Cafeteria?"

CHAPTER SIX:

A Cure for Senioritis

During my last undergraduate semester, I had a very bad case of "senioritis," a condition whereby I neither had solid post-graduation plans nor high motivation to achieve academically. While in my student funk, I enrolled in what I believed to be a very easy set of courses, i.e., 2 Psychology courses, a Public Speaking course, a Geography course, and a beginning Logic course. With minimal effort, I believed I could earn a C+ average for the semester but, by mid-term, I was close to failing all but the 2 Psychology courses.

Operating without having made use of an academic advisor or having read closely the course description, I thought the beginning Logic course was focused on spouting a set of statements such as "All men are mortal. Socrates is a man. Therefore, Socrates is mortal." Hence, I was mystified when my Logic professor discussed Boolean algebra, "logic gates," "truth tables," "circuits," and simplifying algebraic equations A.C. + A.B.C. Having skipped a couple of classes and failing to drop and add a different course in a timely fashion, I was stuck in the Logic class. A few weeks into the term, I also learned how naive I had been in choosing the Geography course.

I based my course selection on my recall of high school geography which consisted of rote memorization of things such as the flags, capitals, birds, flowers, and products associated with American states and select European countries. However, my Geography professor was from Germany, had considerable training in economics, and spent a great deal of time lecturing on the European Common Market. I found myself immersed in highly interdisciplinary material, i.e., the professor's focus on fiscal policy, political economy, trade deficits, and everything but countries' capitals and boundaries.

The Public Speaking course also had unexpected content. Among my Black male friends, rapping, running down lines, and making toasts were signs of being hip. Fast talking "cats" were "hip dudes" who could "sweet talk the babes." Most of my closest friends' verbal skills were so sharp that razors seemed dull. I considered myself to be among the best in running down lines and, with that rich cultural background plus my one UPJ speech course as seemingly great preparation, I decided to take Introduction to Public Speaking.

The Public Speaking professor, Dr. Edwin Black, focused on everything but the forms of eloquence operative in my community. His concept of the great speaker was the person who made the best use of statistics, expert testimony, vivid illustrations, analogies, and, in general, a ton of library research to support one's main contentions. However, the Public Speaking course turned out to be a case of "when life presents you with a lemon, make lemonade" albeit that I was not the maker of the lemonade that "cured" my senioritis.

Anticipating the joy of giving a good speech, I did some library research to ensure that my speeches were steeped in logic, but my most potent rhetorical tool was my rhythmic delivery which mimicked the best I had observed on the parts of Black, fundamentalist, Baptist preachers. I "preached" my speeches in ways that left the students and professor spell bound. My speech on alcoholism brought several students to tears. Dr. Black consistently rewarded me with nothing less than a "B+," and, interestingly in retrospect, never said anything to me about articulation problems as had my UPJ teacher.

During the last month of the term, Dr. Black asked what I planned to do after graduation. I told him that I had been thinking of a civil service career, but was now leaning toward entering the Air Force by way of its officers training program. Privately, I had begun to wonder where civil service would lead me because, after passing an exam, I was notified that I qualified for what seemed to be essentially clerical work at a Philadelphia Naval depot. This prompted me to have second thoughts about having dropped out of the ROTC program, and I met with Air Force recruiting officers to discuss possibilities. Deeply impressed by their presentations and, without telling anyone else, I signed papers I thought only indicated my intentions to attend an officers' training school in Waco, Texas. My understanding was that I could change my mind, if I did so within a month after I graduated. However, it was my professor Dr. Black who was primarily responsible for providing me with a "detour" route to graduate school.

Dr. Black advised that the Air Force would be a terrible waste of my talent and asked me to consider graduate study in his Speech Department. Having taken only one other lower level speech course, I knew nothing about Speech as a formal field of study. My interest was sparked, however, when he informed me that a successful application could lead to full tuition and a stipend of $200 per month, a sum that I had never earned. For that amount of money, a chance to spend more time with Jerri, and hang out a few more years on the college scene, I decided to apply.

As part of the graduate school qualifying process, I took and failed the Miller Analogy examination. A few days later, quite reminiscent of my UPJ admissions, the Department Chair, Dr. Jack Matthews, facilitated my admission to graduate school by providing me with a probationary admission. This time, as a probationary admit, I had to take two summer courses and earn a "B" or higher in each. Still, the notion of again being special based on academic deficiencies bothered me enough to reconsider joining the Air Force.

Being indecisive, I decided to discuss my options with Jerri. As I tried to make the positive case for the Air Force, Jerri listened for a few minutes and declared, "If you choose to go to the Air Force, I can't say that I will be waiting for you to return." I tried to explain with, "I didn't tell you, but before I found out about the graduate fellowship possibility, I'd already signed some papers with the Air Force, but I can change my mind."

Now quite angry, Jerri asked, "You did what? How are we supposed to be a couple, if that's how you're going to make important decisions?" Trying to rationalize my behavior, I replied, "I didn't think it was that big of a deal if I actually went. I'd be away while you were finishing school. You'd graduate, and then we'd be together."

With tears flowing, Jerri shouted, "Well, this ring is no big deal either!" Then she took my ring off her chain, threw it on the ground and, started running toward her dorm. Caught completely off guard and too proud to chase after her, I picked up my ring and headed home to figure out my next steps. Later that day, I went to her room and told her I would enroll in graduate school that summer. She congratulated me for making a good decision, and gave me a big hug. Then she added, "Jack, I didn't insist on graduate school for me. I thought it best for you and, in the long run, us."

After I left the dorm, I reflected on what Jerri said, especially the "best for you and, in the long run, us." It was a deeper side of her that I had failed to realize, and I instantly had greater appreciation for her. I was so relieved to have our relationship restored that I spent the remainder of the term studying longer, harder, and more in-depth than I had ever done in the preceding years. That April, after only two and two-thirds years, I was the recipient of a Bachelor of Science degree in Psychology from the University of Pittsburgh.

A few weeks after graduation, I again found myself in an academic desert with my worthiness to become a full-fledged student being tested. As opposed to courses' content that might be of interest to me, the designated trial-by-fire graduate courses were based on the availability and willingness of the professors to provide me with instruction. As such, the course content was in the area of Communication Disorders, not Rhetoric and Public Address or Communication Research which were my intended areas of concentration. For each class, the professor and I had tiring, three-hour, weekly discussions of the material which I had been assigned.

Actually, my professors were so interested in their subject matter that they did the majority of the talking, periodically asking me probing questions to determine if I understood key concepts from the texts. Although I had no real interest in the material, I worked hard because I wanted to show Jerri that I was now a serious student worthy of a deeper involvement, and I wanted to end my probationary status. My efforts were rewarded with an "A" and a "B+".

Throughout the summer, I had given serious thought to surprising Jerri with not only good grades but also an engagement ring. My plans solidified after a fortuitous encounter with a beleaguered man wearing urine stained pants, a mangy beard and a homeless sign approached me with a jewelry box. "Need a ring? I'll sell it cheap, just fifteen bucks."

After faking a careful look at the silver band with its small diamond, I offered, "Naw man, I only have ten."

"Okay, I'll let you have it for ten, but it's worth a lot more."

"Deal," I answered before he could change his mind.

Believing that at worse I had paid ten dollars for a piece of costume jewelry, I took the ring to the Pitt Book Store salesman responsible for Pitt graduation rings. After looking it over, he surprised me with, "Well, you'd have to take it to an appraiser, but it looks to me to be a fairly good stone." With that information, I was prepared to get engaged.

CHAPTER SEVEN:

Proper Motivation

As Jesse Jackson often stated, "If my mind can conceive it and my heart can believe it, I know I can achieve it." That said, it is also very important to note how difficult it is for one to achieve that which they have never seen and, still worse, have been societally induced to believe they could never achieve! Throughout my undergraduate career, I had never seen a Black professor, Black academic administrator, lawyer, physician, engineer, scientist, corporate manager, banker, public school teacher, or most other professionals whose jobs were a function of having earned one or more college degrees. I had seen one Black female mortician and one Black dentist and, as such, I was a clear case of what is implied by, "Life is like a book. If you never leave home, you never get beyond chapter one."

As an undergraduate, "study abroad" was a non-existent option and, had it existed, I would not have been able to afford such an experience. My only "leaving home" had been going from Johnstown, Pennsylvania to visit my folks "down home" in rural Virginia. Even then, I did not see much because after the stop in Breezewood, Pennsylvania for gas, segregated facilities kept us from stopping again until we reached one of my relative's homes in Goochland County, Virginia. Indeed, crammed in the back seat of a car with several other kids and/or adults and using the local public transportation (buses and street cars only, never a taxi) had been my only modes of transportation. Thus, a new universe was opened for me when Jerri convinced her parents to pay for my first air flight in order to meet me.

Full of excitement, I departed from Pittsburgh, landed in Chicago and, after an hour or so on the ground, flew to San Francisco and then on to Sacramento. Jerri met me at the gate and, after a long-awaited embrace, exclaimed, "Come on! Let's go get your luggage and then you can meet my mom! I've told her so much about you."

Jerri's short, middle-aged mother stood outside a long, steel gray, late model, four-door Cadillac that to my private embarrassment I thought she had rented to impress me. She greeted me with a firm handshake, warm smile, and a friendly, "How are you, Jack? I'm Evelyn's mother. I hope you had a nice flight." I expressed my pleasure in meeting her and tried not to show that this was my first time to have heard Jerri called Evelyn. At the same time, Jerri's mom appeared to be a bit puzzled by my one piece of carry-on luggage, an enlarged gym bag. Once underway, her mother asked, "So, Jack how was school this summer?"

"Oh, I did just fine. My grades were pretty good and my advisor already signed me up for next term." I attempted to impress her by adding, "And my fellowship will pay a $200 monthly stipend, plus all of my tuition."

I was surprised when she made no comment about my stipend and, redirected me with, "I take it that you will be getting your doctorate, not stopping with a master's degree?" I had never considered pursuing the doctorate but, still seeking to impress, I quickly responded with, "Oh yes. I hope to go right through without stopping, maybe even get through early as I did with my undergraduate work."

Jerri interrupted with, "Ma, Jack's been in school all summer. He needs a break from all that. Jack, you promised to take me to a movie on Saturday. Let's go see 'Come Blow your Horn.'" "Fine by me," I exclaimed even though under any other circumstances I would not have gone to see a "girly" love story. I was also pleased that Jerri's comments got me out from under what increasingly appeared to be her mother's not just inquisitive but suspicious eyes.

About fifteen minutes later, we arrived at what looked to me to be a mansion located in a newly developed suburban area. We entered through the ground floor that consisted of a huge fully furnished recreation room, one full and a half bath, bedroom, liquor cabinet, and laundry room. You could smell the rich leather furniture. While I was gawking at the biggest television I had ever seen, Jerri said, "Let's go upstairs. Uncle Sidney stays down here. Let me show you the rest of the house and where you will be sleeping."

On the second floor, I met Jerri's grade school brother and three teenage sisters whose idea of fun was to welcome me with their collective version of Ray Charles' "Hit the road Jack, hit the road Jack, and don't you come back no more, no more…" Jerri's mother stopped them with, "Hey you guys, that's no way to welcome Evelyn's (Jerri's middle name, used by her family and others in Sacramento) guest." Jerri ignored the kids, escorted me to where I would be sleeping which turned out to be a huge bedroom with its own full bath off to the side. Then she continued the tour of her home.

After seeing her parents' master bedroom with its full bath and sitting area, the kids' three bedrooms, the home office, and the expansive kitchen with built-in fixtures, we settled in the living room with its cherry wood paneling, lush carpets, and luxurious furniture. In a span of about fifteen minutes, I had seen more than what I associated with the wealthiest Whites in Johnstown. Prior to my arrival, I had no clue to Jerri's family's affluence, all of which now made me feel extremely insecure.

I was eager to be alone with her, and so I asked Jerri to take me for a walk around the neighborhood. Before she could respond, Jerri's mother said, "Evelyn, you two should be back in about a half hour. Your dad will be here by then." We had barely gotten out of sight of her home when I stopped under a shade tree, pulled out the ring and, without saying a word, put it on her finger. We hugged for the longest time until she said, "I've got to go back to show this to my mom."

I hung back a few steps as Jerri raced into the kitchen and held out her hand for her mother to see the ring. After she stared at me and then ushered Jerri back to her bedroom, I sheepishly went down to the game room. Following what seemed an endless time, Jerri came downstairs, lowered her eyes, gave me the ring, and softly said, "Ma said that's not the way to get engaged, that you have to talk with my father, and some other stuff she wants to do depending on how that goes."

Knowing I was fighting a losing cause, I mildly protested, "Come on Jerri, what's all this? We know how we feel about each other."

"Yeah, but Jack, you don't know my folks and I'm telling you to just hold on to the ring until you talk with my father. Everything will be okay. I've told him a lot about you. Wait a minute. The garage door is going up now. That must be him."

Jerri opened the access door to the garage and I grew weak when I saw her more-than-six-feet-tall, well-groomed father get out of a new sky-blue Lincoln town car. He looked at me and said, "You have to be Jack."

"Yes sir, I am and I am pleased to finally meet you," I said in as strong a voice as possible, and then I rushed over to shake his hand which dwarfed mine. He sat his brief case down and said, "Well, let's go upstairs with the rest of the folks."

Jerri's father greeted his wife and each of his children with a kiss. Then he poured himself a stiff vodka and orange juice drink, picked up the evening paper, and headed outside to read. Given what seemed to be an abrupt shift if not dismissal of me, I asked Jerri about when we might go to the movie, but she suggested that I go talk with her father. It took another ten minutes of stalling before I went into the yard and meekly said, "I need to talk with you about something."

Her father appeared to be bothered by my interruption as he sought to relax, and he dryly asked, "What is it that you need to discuss?"

I remained standing as I told him, "Well, I was thinking about marrying your daughter."

"What do you mean, thinking about?"

"Well, I don't have but so much money. My fellowship pays only $200 a month and maybe we will have to wait..."

He interrupted me with, "Hold on here. Let me tell you something. Whether you marry someone has nothing to do with how much money you have. You get married because you love each other, want to be together for life, and desire to raise a family together, not because of money. If money is your issue, then I can tell you right now that marriage is not for you."

Completely surprised, I responded, "No, what I meant was, I wasn't sure how you might feel about how much I made. I'm not worried. I've gotten by on less."

Her father curtly replied, "I'm not worried about how much you make either." Then he turned the pages of his paper, looked at a section, took a sip of his drink and without looking at me said, "Well, if that's what you guys want to do, its fine by me." He ended the conversation by turning intently to a section of the newspaper, and I went inside, put the ring on Jerri's finger, and told her, "Your daddy is cool with this."

I was everything but cool with my brief interaction with Jerri's father. How could he say money didn't matter when he obviously made far more money than most? My $200 monthly stipend now seemed so small, and I felt small in general. It wasn't that I felt belittled as much as I was perplexed by Jerri's father's statement that the most significant thing I had to offer was my love for his daughter.

Over the next few days, I increasingly realized that I had entered a universe for which there were few comparisons, a universe that I had not conceived of given the lack of Blacks employed by Pitt. Unlike Black students at Pitt today who have the benefit of knowing a Black man as Dean of Pitt's School of Engineering as well as a Black woman as Dean of Education, I was unable to aspire to a level of professionalism for which I could not conceive. Aside from my faculty benefactors in the Speech Communication Department, no other Pitt faculty member had suggested that I might become a professional in any field. It was Jerri's parents' backgrounds that opened new professional vistas for me.

I hadn't a clue regarding what transpired at a historically Black college nor had I heard of a Black person who graduated from an Ivy League Law School. I found out that both of Jerri's parents had graduated from Tuskegee Institute and that her father graduated from Yale law school after serving as a Captain during World War II. He had become so successful with his law practice that one of his tax shelters was a more than 30-acre horse ranch on which he had two homes (one for his family and one for his trainer), bred horses which he raced, and raised cows and pigs primarily for the family's consumption. Moreover, in consequence of his serving as chief legal counsel for the western branch of the NAACP, the family was heavily involved in the civil rights struggle as well as local and state politics, so much so that her father was on a first name basis with the mayor of Sacramento and governor of California.

Although I felt economically out of place, other aspects of the Colley family made me feel right at home and broke down the stereotypes I harbored regarding "uppity Blacks." Their breakfasts routinely included fresh baked biscuits, slab bacon, eggs, and fresh fruit, the things to which I was accustomed. They not only had pork chops smothered with gravy, mashed potatoes, and collards from their garden at the ranch, but her father even drank some of the greens' juice, something I knew as "pot liquor" and had only seen lower class people drink.

After being in Sacramento for a few days, Jerri and I went out to lunch. As soon as the food was served, I asked, "Hey Jerri, why didn't you tell me about the Colley fleet?"

Smiling curiously, she asked, "What fleet?"

"You know the Colley fleet. Your mother has a new Cadillac, your father drives a new Lincoln, your Uncle Sidney drives the ranch station wagon, and we drove here in that no more than two-year-old Camaro that your folks' call the kids' car. If that isn't a fleet, what is?

Plus, your father told me that one of his horses cost more than $50,000 and that's way more than most people earn in a year. So, why didn't you tell me about your family before I came out here?"

Jerri slowed the car and pulled into a parking space. She cut off the engine and, with a disturbed look, said, "Jack, there are few in Sacramento who have not heard of 'Mr. Colley,' the 'Colley family,' and all the stories about 'Mr. Colley' getting big fees for winning huge lawsuits, fighting for civil rights, and what all they think my family owns. A big reason for my going to Pitt was to escape the long shadow of the Colley family and my father in particular. You have no idea what it's like to be 'Evelyn, Nat Colley's daughter'--- instead of me--- just Jerri as you know me. So, no, back at Pitt, I don't talk about my family. If people ask, I tell them that my father is a lawyer and my mother is a housewife who is very involved in the community." Then she added, "You never asked. Part of what I liked about you was that you cared for me without knowing anything about my family."

After further discussion and consuming our lunch, we headed for the movie theater. I watched the screen but my mind was focused on all I had seen and heard about the Colley family. Aside from the material things, I kept recalling an exchange I'd had with her father after he told me, "We're just plain folk up from 'Nowhere, Alabama,' a place where we had to hunt and peck for a living." Puzzled, I asked, "Where exactly was Nowhere?"

Rather proudly, he answered, "Nowhere is Snow Hill, Alabama. And when I tell you it is nowhere, man I mean nowhere. When it got dark, other than our oil lamps that we burned when we had oil, the only lights we had were the moon, the stars, and lightening bugs. We lived miles from the nearest school for Black kids." Then I asked, "And what was this hunting and pecking all about?"

"Jack, I thought you said you were a little bit of a country boy, having lived with your relatives in Virginia. Don't you remember how the chickens went around the yard hunting and pecking for food? We didn't have money to buy chicken feed. Those rascals got big and fat hunting and pecking for worms and bugs or they starved, just like us. We either grew the meat we ate or we went hunting and shot rabbits, squirrels, and sometimes a deer."

As I took in what Jerri's father was saying, I realized that I too was coming up from nowhere, that I too could become a distinguished Black professional. It was being up from nowhere that caused me to balk a little when Jerri and her parents were adamant about a formal wedding taking place in Sacramento. My parents could not afford to attend a California wedding and still with no real understanding of Jerri's parents' resources or their willingness to be of assistance, I thought it best to elope.

Trying to deter her parents, I defiantly suggested getting married on Christmas day. To my total surprise, they immediately seized upon the date and indicated that they would pay all wedding costs, including the cost of flying me, my best man, and Jerri's maid of honor to Sacramento. My family decided that my brother Russell would escort my mother by train to the wedding. My father remained behind to fulfill work obligations as well as to be with my younger brother and sister during the holiday season.

Jerri and I were married December 25, 1963. We spent our honeymoon cleaning a filthy one-bedroom apartment within walking distance of Pitt's campus. It was the only one within walking distance to classes that various Whites were willing to rent to us. Unable to remove all of the yellow stains from the bathtub, I painted it with several coats of white enamel paint. We stuffed rags in the pillow of the living room chair in order to make it usable. Our bed consisted of rusty springs covered by an old mattress.

Although my stipend was increased to $233, we struggled to get by in our "furnished apartment" at a cost of $115 monthly plus utilities. We didn't hit rock bottom because Jerri's parents continued to pay her tuition. They often told us to ask if we were in need, but my pride would not permit me to ask them for financial assistance. Jerri didn't ask because she did not want to further extend the dreaded long shadow of her father to Pittsburgh.

Fortunately, we had only one more year to persevere for Jerri to receive her baccalaureate degree and add to our household finances. Shortly after graduating she was hired by the Department of Public Assistance with an annual salary of $4,200. For me, the Red Sea had parted! More important than our new financial situation was the fact that I had acquired the proper motivation to succeed academically.

I was deeply impressed by the fact that my mother and father-in-law were simply ordinary people from rural Alabama, people just two generations out of slavery, folks who had in many ways richly achieved the American dream while remaining deeply committed to leadership in the civil rights struggle. Observing my wife's parents,

I obtained my first glimpse of how a member of my race could advise the highest elected officials, counsel corporate leaders, and still find time to defend oppressed people. In turn, my motivation to succeed academically was at an all-time high.

CHAPTER EIGHT:

Learning the Discipline

My first semester of full-time graduate study at Pitt was a taxing journey through a never-ending series of doors leading into rooms full of not only new knowledge but also new ways of thinking, talking, and behaving. I was truly a "stranger in a strange land."

Upon entering my first graduate seminar room, my attention was immediately drawn to its all-White male graduate student composition and their dress code. Grey and blue dress slacks, sports jackets, and white or blue dress shirts were the norm. Several of the economically better off third-year guys wore sports jackets with leather patches on the elbows. Later, I observed that all but one of them added neckties on the days they taught introductory undergraduate courses or assisted a professor with teaching an upper level course. The "tieless one" was on the cusp of the 1960s rebellion against institutional norms. He seldom cut his hair, and wore plaid shirts with at least three buttons open, exposing the black curly hair on his chest.

My wardrobe consisted of one dark blue suit reserved for church attendance, funerals and other special events at home. With no money to purchase new clothing and struggling to pay living expenses for me and my new nineteen-year-old bride, I continued to wear my tattered blue jeans, well-worn pull over knit shirts, and one pair of run-down shoes, all of which made me feel like an odd ball among my new peers. I had hoped to receive enough Christmas gift money to purchase two pairs of dress slacks, but I also remained concerned with the possibility of my Black friends teasing me for looking "White" if I wore the new clothing while hanging out with them in the Tuck Shop.

Endlessly drinking black coffee and chain smoking appeared to be the next key aspects of graduate student culture. The seminar room tables were adorned with tobacco pouches, ashtrays, coffee utensils, sugar, dairy creamers, books, and manuscripts. The graduate students proudly paraded into the seminar rooms with their oversized and often badly stained mugs containing black coffee that some laced with sugar. Heavy drinkers often brought a thermos.

Before an experienced graduate student asked a critical question, he would take long drags on his pipe, cigar or cigarette and not utter a word until he had exhaled a large amount of smoke. About to introduce a new major idea, professors tapped their pipes on an ashtray and talked in a most deliberate fashion while slowly filling their pipes with tobacco. Once the pipe was lit, they proceeded to expound some significant idea.

Answering seminar questions seemed ritualistic, necessitating a series of non-verbal actions, with respondents first taking several puffs from their tobacco product, tapping the cigarette or cigar on an ashtray as if to allow time for the nicotine to interact with the brain cells, blowing out the longest possible stream of smoke, frowning a bit while appearing to contemplate, and then holding forth in the most erudite language that one could muster. Without engaging, I was fascinated by the billows of smoke, steaming black coffee, more smoke, and what seemed to be so much pretense consisting of fifteen-letter words flowing freely for hours at a time.

Having spent most of my time in undergraduate classes where professors primarily lectured, my next surprise came when some of the senior graduate students talked as much as the professors and the professors seemingly expected them to do so. More importantly, I hadn't a clue regarding the fact that graduate study consisted of critical analysis, learning and applying research methodologies, theory building, and eventually contributing to knowledge. My concept of learning had progressed little beyond memorization and regurgitation of the facts.

Much of my initial confusion might have been reduced had the Speech Department provided a two-week, "Graduate School 101," summer mini-camp for incoming students to provide an orientation to key theoretical and conceptual frameworks and the basic language of the discipline. It would also have been helpful to have included an orientation regarding the nature of the graduate school teaching and learning processes. Instead, I was left to figure things out for myself, often misunderstanding what was transpiring.

Throughout the first semester, the professors' and students' preferred communication processes and content were as foreign to me as "rapping," "signifying," and "playing the dozens" might have been to them. Their hyperbolic language and convoluted arguments made it extremely difficult for me to decipher the important points being made, so much so that it often seemed as though the dialogue itself was what mattered most. Knowing neither the rules of engagement nor being sufficiently comfortable with the content of the discussions for most of the first term, I simply observed the seminar rituals. As they drank, puffed and pontificated, I remained alert for the professors' indication of the criteria that would be used to grade us in order that I might earn the "B" average associated with keeping my tuition scholarship and stipend.

Gradually, it became clear that my peers and professors placed a premium on being "learned" and, as such, they used an array of non-English derived words for rather common terms. Ethical, emotional and logical appeals were replaced with Aristotle's concepts of ethos, pathos, and logos. Engaging in such word games appeared to be substitutes for being profound, with professors referring to "epideictic and deliberative" forms of oratory as opposed to more commonly used communication terms, "ceremonial and argumentative." I was taught that there were good guys, "rhetoricians," seeking the truth about nearly everything, and bad guys, "sophists," exploiting other people for selfish ends. The most peculiar term for me was "topoi" which was used to refer to lines of argument.

As undergraduates, we took an array of multiple choice, true or false, and essay tests. Occasionally, term papers were assigned in senior level classes. Therefore, it came as a total surprise to me that extensive reading, writing and discussing scholarly papers were the principal means for learning in graduate school. I also did not know that, having presented one's paper, engaged in intense debate, and having revised one's manuscript, the next goal was to transform a seminar paper into a convention paper and, ultimately, publish it in a national journal. It was not until half way through the first term that I had ever heard of the national Speech Communication Association, its refereed journals, and its scholarly convention.

Lacking understanding of the process for building a body of scholarly literature, I viewed scholarly publications as similar to notches on the handle of a gunslinger's pistol, only in this instance it represented evidence of a sharp scholar as opposed to a sharp shooter. It was years later that I learned that most of the White graduate students had not only been mentored by their undergraduate professors, but also that most of them had been referred to a particular tenured Pitt professor(s) who continued to mentor them throughout their graduate study. I was more like a waif who had been given temporary shelter but then left on his own to survive.

After my first graduate semester, I was reminded of a story about thousands of caterpillars climbing on top of each other, crushing each other, as they all climbed to the top of their self-made hill. Along the way, some fell to their deaths. Many collapsed after climbing several days without food, water or rest. Frustrated by the entire ordeal, others committed suicide. Finally, one weary caterpillar descending from the very top was met by an aspirant just beginning his trek. The one going up inquired about what was at the top, and the beleaguered one coming down, grimaced and grumbled, "Nothing!" Yet, thousands and thousands of caterpillars continued their struggle to get to the top. Surely, something must be up there if so many were trying so hard to get to the top.

As my professors and peers continued to pile more and more abstract words upon each other, I developed serious doubts regarding what was at the top of the Speech Communication curriculum. I kept climbing because of the free tuition, $233 monthly stipend, the commitment to my wife to pursue a graduate degree, the unwavering support of my family, and the lack of a viable alternative. Without realizing what was taking place, however, I slowly got pulled into the graduate student culture.

I was first encouraged to climb faster because of the student feedback I received when I presented my paper on Martin Luther King Jr.'s "I Have a Dream" speech. My six or seven pages of "wisdom" focused on the symbolic and actual importance of dreams in the African American community and, hence, King's excellent strategic choice of a title for his speech. During my oral presentation, I noted that dreams, for many Blacks, were not 'just dreams.' My mother, her mother, and most older Blacks knew the symbolic importance of dreams. A select few were notorious interpreters of dreams and prescribed behavioral responses based on the content of dreams. For example, if you dreamed about death, they would tell you that the appropriate lottery number to play was 697. And the most powerful dream was one in which God spoke to the dreamer, thereby imbuing the dreamer with a bit of supernatural power.

Smoke swirled and my classmates expressed so many insights that I simply listened, for about forty minutes, as they debated aspects of my presentation. They spent more time discussing my paper than any other paper that term. Initially, I thought there was a bit of patronage based on the fact that I was the only Black in the class. However, after several students requested copies of the final version of the paper, I too began to believe there was something very special about the paper. I thought I had reached some level of "academic nirvana" when my professor requested that I come to his office for further discussion of the paper.

Approaching my professor's office, my heart was pounding from the excitement associated with the possibility of him suggesting that my paper be submitted for a convention presentation and subsequent publication. Once in his office, however, it sank to a sluggish pace when he said, "This is a very good paper, but I will not grade it for content until you first address some very serious writing problems." He handed me the paper. On several pages, I noted that dreadful red ink.

After reading some of my professor's comments pertaining to spelling, grammar, and style, I felt so ashamed and quickly said, "I'll have this back to you in a few days." Frowning, my professor cautioned, "No, take your time. The paper requires considerable work. It would be tragic if your great thoughts were so poorly presented that you received a poor grade." I meekly replied, "Okay." and left his office. My growing nausea reminded me of that dreadful morning when I awoke after a night of celebrating a friend's 18*th* birthday with shots of Old Crow and several cans of beer.

I resubmitted the paper three times before it was assigned a "B." This ordeal rocked my sense of preparedness for further graduate study, shook my self-esteem, and induced a feeling of inferiority based on my perceptions of the other students' intellectual abilities. Full of doubt, I again wondered if there might be little or nothing at the top of the Speech Communication hill or, actually, I had too many cognitive deficits to comprehend what was up there, much less get there. My intellectual self-esteem underwent further assault when I received a "B-"and more negative writing comments on a paper in a second seminar.

I had learned that, for the most part, only "A's," "B's," and "C's" were given in graduate school, with a "C" essentially being a failing grade. In the long run, however, it proved quite beneficial that my one professor, Dr. Black, made me rewrite all of the papers that I submitted to him. In addition, my wife read and commented on what seemed to be endless drafts of my papers. My grades improved and, by the end of the year, I was receiving "B+" and "A-" grades.

Three weeks into the new term, a major disaster struck. The Departmental secretary informed me that my advisor wanted me to come to his office as soon as possible. When I arrived, the reddish hue of his face signaled bad news for me. Staring at the floor, he spoke very softly, almost timidly, as he indicated that he and the Department chairman had received numerous complaints from the students in my Introduction to Public Speaking course. Then, looking sadly at me, he added that he was fearful of my losing my graduate fellowship, since it required me to teach that class as well as perform some grading duties for a class he taught.

After I asked about the nature of the students' complaints, he said, "Well, now, they are not complaining so much about your competence and that's a good thing. However, they report that, well, I don't know another way to put it other than you sound ignorant when you talk. They also said they sometimes can't understand what you are saying because of the way you pronounce certain words." I wanted to leave the room but my hurt feelings bogged down my ability to think and act. I didn't know if my all-White students were reacting to differences in my speech or actual deficiencies. Perhaps they were primarily reacting to the fact that I might have been their first Black teacher. Also weighing heavily on me was the bit about the possible loss of my financial support.

My professor broke the silence with, "Now, there is a way we can address the way you talk, and you will be able to keep your fellowship." However, he plunged me deeper in emotional distress when he added, "I want you to make an appointment with a therapist in the Department's Speech Clinic. Here is her name and number. She has agreed to immediately fit you into her schedule."

It was truly humiliating to be informed that something was so wrong with me that a therapist had agreed to see me immediately, as if I had some kind of infectious disease. Back home, my friends would have thought I was certified crazy, a deviant, or some worse form of defective humanity had I made known that I was being referred to a therapist. I certainly had to keep secret the fact that I needed a therapist. The stigma regarding therapy dwelled in the same mad house as homophobia in my community. However, knowing that I could not afford to lose my graduate funding and feeling too low to discuss the matter, I meekly agreed to make the appointment and left my advisor's office. Privately, I decided to make a final decision after talking with my wife.

I knew Jerri's college-educated parents were adamant about their children's use of proper spoken and written language. Since none of them sounded "White" when they talked, I looked forward to discussing with her whether I should meet with the therapist.

After I told her about the criticism of my speech, she diplomatically advised, "Jack, I know you're comfortable with your speech. They might not understand you, but I do. I think you should do as they say for a while, and show them that you can speak both ways." Her advice provided me with an acceptable solution and, knowing I had no other choice, I agreed to make my first clinic appointment.

When I saw the therapist on the first day, I was angered by the fact that she was a White graduate student in the Speech Pathology section of the Department. I had assumed that I would be seeing a private clinician. Now, I wondered whether other graduate students knew about my situation and how long it would take before some of my friends found out that I was "in therapy." Noticing the grimace on my face, the therapist exclaimed, "Come on Jack. Things aren't that bad." I gave a rather dry "sure" and followed her into her office.

As a diagnostic technique, my therapist had me talk for a half hour. Temporary relief came when she told me to come back in two days, after she had analyzed my speech. When I returned, she informed me that I had an "i" "e" substitution problem whereby I pronounced "Center" Avenue as "Cinter" Avenue. Smiling, she said, "When your tongue is especially lazy, you say 'Sinner' Avenue." Although she spared me of the possibility that my lips were somehow too thick, my mind was buzzing with anger and confusion.

I could hear the difference in sounds when she pronounced the words, but when I tried to articulate the differences, it took about ten attempts for me to hear myself distinguish between "Center," "Cinter," and "Sinner" Avenue. Gradually, over several sessions with my therapist, the differences became clearer and I wondered how I ever failed to make the distinction. Nevertheless, I was very hesitant to swap "Center" for "Cinter" or "Sinner" because I did not want to sound as White, prim and proper as my therapist.

After practicing for a half hour each day over several weeks and showing signs of improvement with the "e" "i" issue, my therapist indicated that she needed to talk with me about another set of articulation problems. According to her, I systematically dropped the final "g" from words such as "going" and "coming," pronouncing them as "goin" and comin." This time, I offered no resistance. I just wanted to take what seemed to be the bad medicine that was supposedly good for me and be done. It couldn't be worse than the cod liver oil my mother gave us to "clean us out" each winter and spring.

Like the psychologically broken Winston in George Orwell's 1984, I was worn down and willing to see, hear, and speak whatever my therapist requested of me. Hence, I quickly complied with her next suggested corrections of things such as "two desses" instead of "two desks" or three "tesses" instead of three "tests." Trying to make light of the situation, she also indicated that I "gobbled up" "r" and said "befoe" instead of "before." Performing her best imitation of me, she added, "Befoe I put the tesses on the students' desses, I was goin to explain the rules" is not the way a graduate student instructor should talk."

Listening to my therapist's imitation of my speech, for the first time, I considered the possibility that my students might rightfully think of me as ignorant. Mentally confused and seeking to rationalize my increasingly compliant behavior, I began to tell myself that perhaps many of my people endured so many hardships not because of what Whites did to them but because they were very ignorant as evidenced by the way they talked. Hence, I was less bothered when my therapist told me there was yet one more set of speech issues to be addressed.

According to my White students, I used a lot of "unprofessional" language in class. An example was that I used phrases such as "I'm hip" to indicate my understanding of something a student said. My therapist recommended that this and other phrases as "Dig this" and "Dig it" not be used in class, lest the students think that I was not being professional. Trying to be funny, I said, "Okay, I dig where you bees comin' from and so I'll be coolin' it in class." Her hesitant laugh and stare made me wonder if she got the humor or believed that I had not gotten her message since she considered our therapy sessions to be professional occasions for which my comments were inappropriate, regardless of my intent.

After another month of making considerable progress with the designated changes in my speech patterns, my advisor informed me that the students had ceased making critical comments and, indeed, several were now praising my instruction. I became increasingly comfortable with my new articulation patterns until I visited Terrace Hall, a favorite bar for Black graduate students and young professionals who wanted to remain connected to their community roots. I arrived after the kickoff for a Monday Night Football game, and greeted my friends with, "What's happening with all of you folks down here on Center Avenue?"

My emphatic "g" on "happening" and my pronunciation of "Center" was so unusual that my friends immediately started laughing. I could not figure out the reason for the laughter until one of them asked me to repeat what I had said. When I did, I too heard an articulation pattern that was foreign to the Terrace Hall community. Throughout the night when I slipped and made additional use of my new articulation patterns, I continued to be ridiculed for what my friends termed "Jack's new proper, Pitt, White folks way of talking." One guy, Ben, teased, "Man, what are those folks doin to you, Brotha Man, down on the Pitt plantation? Can ya'll believe this Negro, Center Avenue! I guess he'll quit eatin chitlins."

Quickly regaining my community sensibilities, I countered with, "Don't worry as long as yo mama still eats chitlins!" Ben faked a punch to my face, laughed, and said, "Well, you still can git down with the dozens. Let me git you a beer, Bro."

The next morning, I dwelled on my very complicated dilemma. Whites determined that my home language rendered me ignorant and nonprofessional. Hearing my altered speech, my friends accused me of trying to become White, frowning upon my roots. To further complicate matters, I had begun to like my new way of talking on campus because I thought I sounded more intelligent, that my new way of talking was not White but right. And when I listened to my friends on the bar, although they sounded hip, they did sound a bit ignorant. However, I valued their friendship as well as how they perceived me, and I decided that my therapy days were over.

Several days later, I arranged to meet with my therapist. As soon as she closed the door, I blurted out, "I am not going to attend another therapy session!" After I related the Terrace Hall incident, she offered, "Jack, think about those people for a minute. 'Those people' aren't going very far. 'Those people' are not in graduate school, with all of the possibilities that you have for a career. 'Those people' are simply jealous of you."

My mind flashed back to the first time I set foot on the UPJ campus and the secretary made reference to "you people." Now, as if a hysterical, wicked shrew was bellowing in my ear, "those people" became increasingly loud and painful. My therapist didn't know "those people" who were in fact the vanguard of an emerging Black middle class. "Those people" were my people! "Those people" had achieved professionally. Whether she meant anything racist or not, I interpreted "those people" as a reference to "ignorant niggers" and, sadly, having learned to switch an "e" for an "i" and add "t" to "tes," momentarily I too had thought "those people" were "ignorant niggers." Frustrated and flabbergasted, I left my therapist's office without saying a word but privately vowed to never again attend a speech therapy session, no matter what it cost me.

When I informed my advisor of my decision to end the therapy, he indicated his disappointment with my choice, but that he understood the reason for my decision. To my surprise, he added, "I have been listening to you and I have noticed a real change. I believe you can work this out on your own. You keep up the good work and I will see to it that you don't lose your fellowship." I felt so relieved that he seemed to understand me. At least I wanted to believe that to be true in this academic environment where I was perceived to be a linguistic cripple.

Years later, when I studied Sociolinguistics and learned that Black English patterns merely reflected different dialects as opposed to mental deficiencies, I came to resent even more the roles my therapist, I, and my professors played in causing me to temporarily accept racist views of the English spoken by me and others. It angered me to find out that my professors knew that, in the 1949 Africanisms in the Gullah Dialect, Lorenzo Turner documented the survival of African languages' vocabulary, grammar, syntax and intonation patterns in the variety of English spoken by slave descendants, making their rule governed language different not deficient.

I especially resented the fact that not one of my professors informed me that, also in 1949, S.I. Hayakawa wrote <u>Language in Thought and Action</u>, a book that dealt extensively with the fact that linguistically speaking there is no such thing as "correct" or "incorrect," "right" or "wrong" articulation. Instead, "right" and "wrong" were always a matter of what was deemed socially and politically acceptable by those empowered to make such determinations.

Neither my therapist nor my professors ever discussed with me why powerful Whites accepted and often praised varieties of English spoken by Whites across the United States. I had to figure it out for myself why John Kennedy and Lyndon Johnson as well as others could articulate differently yet become the chief executive officer of the largest corporation in the world. However, my articulation differences led to an assault on my cognitive capacities as well as my psychological and economic well-being.

Neither my professors nor my therapist suggested that my spoken language was different as opposed to deficient. Through my own subsequent studies, I learned that racist ideology held that I had a "thick lazy tongue" in keeping with my "thick brain," but some Whites had "beautiful, thick German" accents while other Whites spoke with "romantic French" accents. My professors could have helped end such racism by teaching all students that difference in speech patterns are reflective of historical, geographical and social differences as in the case of Black English speakers or international teaching assistants, not automatically equated with linguistic deficiencies. Unfortunately for me and many others, it took several subsequent generations of new scholars to address these biases. For a good part of my graduate student days, therefore, I remained enmeshed in a very frustrating schizophrenic existence.

As I increasingly switched language when talking with my friends as opposed to members of the Department, I came to know intimately what W. E. B. DuBois meant when he wrote about a psychological burden imposed on many Blacks, i.e., "It is a peculiar sensation, this double consciousness, this sense of always looking at one's self through the eyes of others, of measuring one's soul by the tape of a world that looks on in amused contempt and pity. One ever feels his twoness –an American, a Negro; two warring souls, two thoughts, two unreconciled strivings; two warring ideals in one dark body, whose dogged strength alone keeps it from being torn asunder."

My soul wanted to keep things that nourished it: savory morsels of soul food; "trash talkin" with my homeboys; "foot stompin" in those sing-song sermons, "amen-sayin" churches; "worshipin" of a God "dat" don't never change; being relaxed by Ray Charles' and Aretha Franklin's rhythm and blues; observing how my parents and other old saints' "made a way outta no way;" hearing "Shine" type legends told by my favorite uncles; and every "goin" and "comin" I ever said comfortably.

Simultaneously, aspects of my graduate school environment became increasingly attractive to me. I enjoyed teaching my Public Speaking classes for which I received improved teaching ratings each term. The seminar room increasingly ceased being a world of words for the sake of words after I prepared a paper on Black's use of storytelling for didactic purposes. "Pathos" made more sense when I related it to the preaching styles in the churches I had known.

As I developed intellectual interests in sociolinguistics, ethnography, and political rhetoric, I didn't conceive of this as wanting to "turn White" in any way. I desired to make connections between my esoteric classroom learning and issues of social, economic, and political relevance to members of my community. Just such a connection took place when I first heard references to "Black is beautiful." I recall saying to myself, "Wow, that's the persuasive definition thing Charles Stevenson discussed in his book on values and ethics!"

"Black is beautiful" was a persuasive definition that gave a new emotive meaning to a familiar word without changing substantially its conceptual meaning, and it was being done to change the directions of *my* people's interests. Knowing that my people were in need of so many persuasive definitions regarding their language, dress, color, body shapes, hair, lips, and everything else about them that White racism rendered inferior, my imagination was sparked regarding the relevance of my studies to the improvement of my people.

Most importantly, I came to understand that Blacks need not carry the burden of double consciousness, especially when this means "White is right, superior, or better than Black." I could in fact be "unapologetically Black when and where I enter." As a graduate student in 1965, I came to know what my college sophomore granddaughter, Akili, knew in 2018, i.e., that, as a price of being a professional, I need not first affirm White cultural norms, that it is one thing to be practical in terms of coping in a White dominated society, but this neither requires acceptance of the White hegemonic situation nor debasement of self. As my high school grandsons, Javon and Deven also told me, "most Black kids have a White voice they use to get desirable outcomes in their suburban public school" but they in no way view their Black language or themselves as inferior.

CHAPTER NINE:

The Dawning of Black Consciousness

From grade school through graduate school, no teacher ever required that I read a book written by anyone other than a White person. In preparation for an undergraduate assignment and, given publicity about the civil rights movement, the one book I selected and read in its entirety was Martin Luther King Jr.'s Strides Toward Freedom. I reached adulthood having never been taught nor made an effort to learn about the history of my race and, like so many other mis-educated Blacks, I knew only negative stereotypes about Africa. It took the radical upheavals of the 1960s to awaken my racial, social, cultural and political consciousness.

I watched the nation's White "flower children" making their counter-culture, "turning on" to psychedelic drugs, espousing utopian concepts of peace, and exploring new sexual mores while "turning off" the establishment. Their actions left me wondering why I should be so eager to gain entry into the White America they detested. After observing White student protests against the Viet Nam War and the military-industrial-complex, I wondered why I had once been so eager to join the military.

My budding race consciousness and increasingly radical thinking was fed by television's graphic accounts of White police officers using vicious dogs, water hoses, cattle prods, clubs, horses, and other forms of government sanctioned physical abuse against my people in the South ---people who merely wanted to vote, attend public educational institutions, eat in public restaurants, or drink from public water fountains reserved for Whites only. If anyone had harbored doubts regarding the extent to which racism was officially sanctioned, Alabama Governor George C. Wallace clarified things in his 1963 inaugural address: "In the manner of the greatest people that have ever trod this earth, I draw the line in the dust and toss the gauntlet before the feet of tyranny… segregation today...segregation tomorrow...segregation forever." His words chilled me to the bone and caused me to fear traveling anywhere near Alabama.

The depth of the evil resolve sordid minds had to continue the legacy of American slavery and segregation was underscored by the horrible 1963 Birmingham church bombing that killed four children and two others. Ku Klux Klan members defiantly murdered James Chaney, Andrew Goodman, and Michael Schwerener in 1964, and the failure to prosecute them made it very clear that justice had a special form of blindness that favored White criminals.

Angered by the almost daily unfolding horrors and, absent any formal courses that focused on Black Americans, a small "consciousness-raising" group of Pitt students began meeting informally to discuss race-related current events and literature. We started by reading the Autobiography of Malcolm X. His transformation from criminal to militant Black Muslim leader impressed us as we sought to change ourselves from "irrelevant Negro college students" to "conscious Black students."

In his The Souls of Black Folk, Dubois reinforced our perceived seriousness of race problems with his prophetic statement, "The problem of the twentieth century is the problem of the color-line, —the relation of the darker to the lighter races of men in Asia and Africa, in America and the islands of the sea."

We absorbed everything we could obtain from the speeches of Stokely Carmichael, Angela Davis, H. Rap Brown, Maulana Ron Karenga, Huey P. Newton, Malcolm X, Martin Luther King Jr., and others propagating direct action against racism. Repeating their slogans related to "Black power," "burn baby burn," "its nation time," "we want it all, here and now," and "power to the people," were incantations propelling me to action. Before the end of the semester, we had become the Afro-American Cultural Society (AACS).

We AACS members secured and repeatedly played recordings such as Malcolm X's "Message to Grass Roots." Regarding Martin Luther King Jr. and others locking arms and singing "We Shall Overcome," I loved the way Malcolm X responded with, "You don't do that in a revolution. You don't do any singing. You're too busy swinging." Another favorite passage was his criticism of suffering peacefully when attacked by a racist. Malcolm declared, "If he puts a hand on you, send him to the cemetery." Although I wasn't prepared to send anyone to the cemetery or do anything to have myself sent, Malcolm X's rhetoric did help push me closer to becoming an "activist" as opposed to a "liberal" who as someone said, "discussed and discussed and discussed until it all became disgusting."

We got really pumped by Malcolm X's presentation of the house and field Negroes' reactions to the possibility of escaping from the slave plantations. The house Negro said, "Where you going to find a better place than this?" The field Negro said, "Any place is better than this." After first hearing the speech, I and others mockingly began to refer to the "Pitt Plantation." Eventually, as self-declared "field Negroes," we perceived the need to go beyond our campus discussions and do something in the "real world."

Initially, the AACS focused on the problem of public school segregation. We were split between the view that segregation was wrong under any circumstances, as opposed to leaving the schools segregated but providing the African American schools with equal resources. Some of us began to refer to desegregation as "disintegration" of what we now more often called our Black community. As we became increasingly separatists in our thinking, we settled on the compromised view that Blacks should be able to attend their neighborhood schools, but that a separate Black school with appropriate resources could not only be separate and equal, but separate and superior.

Although I allied myself with the separate and superior group, I felt hypocritical and conflicted. Privately, I reminded one AACS member that I was provided the chance to attend the essentially all-White University of Pittsburgh at Johnstown, not a historically Black college. Now, like him, I was enrolled in an all-White graduate program. Without these bits of good fortune, I would not be attending AACS meetings. Subsequently, I had no further discussion of this topic with him or the majority of the AACS members who became increasingly critical of integration as they became inextricably bound to their newly found version of Black pride.

I did find comfort in discussions with my wife who too believed in Black pride but, as was the case with her NAACP parents, favored integration. She never engaged in the more radical race-related discourse, never used terms such as "whitey," and never advocated violent approaches to solving societal problems. As she often said to me back then and to this day, "We are stronger as a country if we work together with a willingness to listen and consider different people's perspectives. These schools and this country belong to all of us." Although I agreed with her, still I did not have the courage to defend my positive views of Pitt when meeting with the AACS.

Adding to my sense of guilt was the fact that I knew I had no intention of transferring to a historically Black college or university even though I knew there were Speech Communication programs at institutions such as Howard University, Jackson State University, Morgan State University, and Texas Southern. My thinking at the time still held that I was in a higher quality program even though I knew next to nothing about the programs at the historically Black institutions.

I was guilty of the 1960s criticism, "He who tries to convince others about their Blackness, appears to be together. He who convinces himself is together." During these earliest stages of developing our Black consciousness, the mere rhetoric of revolution was sufficient heady wine. Reciting Claude McKay's "If We Must Die" was enough "action" for me. By merely reading radical literature, I felt I was "fighting back" even though I had no experience with racists physically attacking me as McKay wrote in the following lines: "If we must die, let it not be like hogs, hunted and penned in an inglorious spot, ...like men we'll face the murderous, cowardly pack, pressed to the wall, dying, but fighting back!"

Absent the formal courses universities eventually created related to the Black American experience, we forged our Black consciousness as best we could. For example, one day after listening to Stokely Carmichael talk about "honkified minds," "Handkerchief Head Hubert Humphrey," "Uncle Tom Negroes," and what the White man had done to Native Americans and African slaves, I wanted to become as Black as possible, to become a bonafide Black militant. Naively, I began by growing what became a two-inch, seldom combed, crop of hair known then as an "Afro." This "action" was followed by other trappings such as my red, black, and green dashiki; a very dark pair of Ray Charles sunglasses; and a pair of black combat boots.

My "Black Power" handshake morphed into five rapid moves that ended with me snapping my fingers and pounding my fist on my chest. "Brother," "Sister," the Arabic "Asalamm Alaikum" and the Swahili "Hu Jumbo" were used to greet other "conscious brothers and sisters" on campus. After being baptized in these symbolic notions of Black consciousness, my attention turned to more substantive matters such as the content of my academic studies.

The required master's thesis provided another opportunity for me to make what I considered to be a very radical step. I decided to do something related to the needs of my people instead of studying a White male from Greek and Roman antiquity or early American history as was typically done by the other graduate students. To my surprise and their credit, the increasingly socially conscious faculty members enthusiastically agreed with me.

My 1965 study, "Negroes' Perceptions of White People's Sincerity," identified verbal cues we used to determine a White speaker's sincerity. The indices of insincerity consisted of a number of stereotypical phrases, one of the most offending being the use of "you people" as a collective term for Blacks. Other indications of insincerity were, "Show me the latest dance." "I really think colored people are cool." "I have a lot of respect for you people." "I think Willie Mays was the greatest." "What exactly does the Negro want?" "One of my best friends is a Negro." All of these statements were viewed as patronizing. Notwithstanding my growing Black consciousness, I didn't take note of the fact that I used "Negroes" instead of "Blacks" throughout the manuscript.

After the completion of my thesis, I continued to find ways to modify the nature of my graduate education, to counter what I thought to be efforts to mis-educate me. For example, I did my best to avoid the doctoral requirement to pass two foreign language examinations, arguing that the European languages were not relevant to my pursuit of what I had begun to call Black Communication. Since Pitt did not offer a major in any African language, I argued that the requirement should be waived for me. My faculty committee and I settled for graduate work in statistics counting as a neutral foreign language, but that could not be the one in which I earned high proficiency.

My advisor informed me that the Russian psychologists were doing work of interest to me. After listening to him for a half hour and realizing there was no escaping the requirement, I agreed to take Russian. My added rationalization was that Russia was "radical" with its communism, even though I knew nothing substantively about communism.

I labored through a year of learning first the Cyrillic alphabet and then a considerable amount of Russian vocabulary, grammar and syntax. We primarily read articles related to natural science research until, one evening after class, I told the professor that the content was not related to my academic pursuits and asked him to provide more relevant articles. During the next class, he gave us an article that referred to Abraham Lincoln having led a revolution of the American proletariat. It left a lasting impression on me regarding the power of authors to define reality.

Eventually, I earned the requisite score for high proficiency in reading scientific Russian, opening the door for the conduct of my doctoral dissertation. As one of the most depressed Pittsburgh communities during the late 1960s, the nearby Hill District was a perfect laboratory for me. With the full support of the faculty, I decided to investigate the relative effectiveness of communication between poor people in the Hill District with Black and White middle class professionals as compared to Black indigenous non-professionals. .

I conceptualized the research problem as a cross-cultural communication situation emanating from differences in language, values, and beliefs between the "culture of poverty" and the "middle class professional culture." For example, the research literature documented the fact that many middle class professionals viewed sex as something to be delayed until marriage. Many poor people considered sex to be one of life's few free pleasures. Hence, the professionals' admonitions related to chastity often fell on deaf ears. How could one possibly take seriously the advice of someone who knew so little about one's daily realities?

To become known by the people whom I wanted to interview, I spent the months of April and May as a door to door volunteer worker interviewing Hill District residents regarding their needs for social services. My volunteer time had the unanticipated result of enhancing my race consciousness and behavior. My "poor graduate student status" paled in comparison to the hunger, despair, untreated diseases, youth pregnancies, unemployment, slum housing, and crime that I observed. I was reminded of the saying, "I wept because I had no shoes until I met someone who had no feet," and therefore I continued to volunteer for a second month instead of collecting data.

On one occasion, I noticed a child banging his head against the kitchen wall, rocking and talking very little. The mother was worried and confused, but had no health insurance. She was also afraid, as she stated, "to go down there, dressed in these old clothes, and ask all those big shots to help my child. Some of them got too much education for me and don't seem to really want to be bothered --they just be earning their checks."

I convinced the mother to go with me to the nearby Poverty Program office, and introduced her to people who in turn secured free medical help for the child. It was quite rewarding when I saw the child playing outside about a month later and the mother gave me a big hug for helping. Subsequently, I became so involved with convincing residents to make use of the social services that, for much of the summer, I forgot about my dissertation and only returned to it when my advisor asked me about my progress. Now, conducting interviews proved to be a snap because people were willing to help "the brother from Pitt" finish his college work. By the middle of August, I had become the "all but dissertation completed" doctoral student ready to assume his first faculty position.

Before leaving Pitt, it was not lost on me that the focus of my thesis and dissertation was a function of my self-directed interests related to Blacks, not anything that my professors provided me during my graduate studies. I had yet to come to grips with notions such as my professors having a "Eurocentric" focus, that their preeminent theory and research ideas were those derived from Europe, particularly ancient Rome and Greece. Aristotle's and Plato's theories of rhetoric reigned supreme. All of the "great speakers" were White males. My professors never presented content and related research methods for studying speech communication in Black communities. When it came to the latter, I was the "professor."

CHAPTER TEN:

The New Black Faculty Member On a Historically White Campus

When I began to pursue a full-time faculty position for the 1967-68 academic year, I did not know the existence of the extensive personal and professional networks White faculty members had among themselves. Nor did I know that these networks were used extensively when doctoral students applied for faculty positions. I had a faculty advisor who approved the courses I took each term as well as monitored my progress in meeting graduation requirements. However, I did not have a mentor, much less a sponsor, who helped pave the way for me to acquire a faculty position by making direct contact with his White colleagues seeking to fill positions at other institutions. Hence, I was baffled when I heard one of my student peers discuss the various "offers" he had received without having gone through a formal application process.

Absent a sponsor, I was left to participate in what graduate students termed the "meat market," i.e., the job placement services of the national Speech Communication Association. Students sent their resumes to the Association; the resumes were put on file; and those seeking to fill positions often interviewed top candidates during the Association's national convention, usually held in November. Other potential candidates were contacted via mail and asked to submit letters of reference.

At the end of February, I had received no invitations to submit letters of reference much less an invitation to be interviewed. Finally, in late April, I received an invitation for an interview at Central Michigan University (CMU) located in rural north-central Michigan. Essentially, a late April invitation meant that CMU had not been able to fill their vacant position since most positions were filled much earlier.

One possible reason that the Central Michigan position had not been filled was that the job description required a rare combination of teaching and research competencies, i.e., someone to teach [1] graduate courses in Experimental Methods in Speech Communication as well as The Psychology of Speech; [2] undergraduate courses in General Semantics as well as the Introduction to Public Speaking course; [3] pursue one's research; and [4] engage in service to the Department. This was a very rare set of competencies at that time because "experimental methods" was new to the discipline and "general semantics" was on its way out of the discipline.

In terms of "location, location, location," CMU was located in Mount Pleasant, Michigan --one of the least desirable places to live. This tiny rural community had no major department stores. Folks still purchased clothing from mail order catalogues. Temperatures in the teens were normal during the winter. The water was so "hard," so full of minerals that the water had an awful rotten egg type odor. Folks drove miles to obtain drinking water from a spring bubbling out of a mountainside.

Except for the handful of Black students on campus, the local community was essentially all White. During my one-year stay, I never saw another Black family in the area. Nevertheless, after my campus interview, I received and accepted my one and only job offer to serve as an Assistant Professor for what I thought to be a very large salary of $8,500 per year.

The harsh physical environment and challenging racial climate not only made the CMU year a true hardship tour but also one that enhanced the development of my racial consciousness. Especially trying was the racial naiveté of the CMU students, faculty and administration. On one occasion, a frail, grey-haired White faculty member slowly walked up to me at the new faculty reception and said proudly, "Aha, Bantu, right?" After I looked puzzled and didn't respond verbally, he said, "Darn. I must have gotten it wrong. When I was in Africa, I could easily identify most people by their tribes. Where are you from?" I said, "Pittsburgh" and, looking puzzled, he asked, "Well, what tribe are you and how long were you in Pittsburgh?" He continued to try to identify my African tribal identity until I walked away without responding further to him. He was not alone in terms of insisting that I was an African.

After teaching my first week, I attended the Saturday football game. During the game, several groups of White students came by my section, stopped, waved toward me, chatted among themselves, and then left. After class on Monday, a blushing White female student met me in the hall and asked shyly why I had not waved back at her and her friends on Saturday. I indicated that I hadn't recognized them, and she gushed forth with, "I brought them by to see my professor who was an African prince!"

I asked how she knew I was an African prince, and she said, "That was easy. I had seen your picture in a copy of a recent National Geographic. There was a picture of you, your tribe, and a story about how you had gotten a college education in America." Privately a bit amused, I decided not to shatter her sense of reality and stated, "Well, I have to get to my next class." It seemed that it would have taken too long and been too agonizing to try and unpack the stereotypes she apparently held.

An incident while having dinner at a White CMU faculty member's home provides additional insight to the racial isolation in Mt. Pleasant, Michigan. Things went well for the first fifteen minutes of pleasantries, at which time the couple's five- or six-year-old child came into the room, stared at my wife Jerri, and then gradually approached her. When he got within reach, he stuck his finger in his mouth, dampened it, and then rubbed his wet finger on Jerri's leg. As we adults stared, the child declared, "Humm, its chocolate and it doesn't come off." Jerri replied with a smile, "No, it doesn't come off. I am this color and you are your color." Immediately, the mother dragged the child by one arm out of the room, slammed a bedroom door, and did something that led to the child screaming and crying.

The embarrassed father told us that neither he nor his wife had any issues with color, how sorry he was for what his child had done, and that he had no explanation for his child's conduct other than the possible negative influence of other children at school. When the distraught mother returned, she too apologized profusely.

Jerri again tried to ease the tension by offering, "That's why they are kids. They are still learning." The father then nervously suggested that we go to the table and begin dinner. Unfortunately, we all now lacked appetites and we ate while making only occasional and forced comments. Finally, I indicated that I would skip desert, Jerri noted that it was getting late, and we decided to leave.

The kind of racial ignorance I encountered at CMU did not end there. Decades later I was a tenured faculty member and Vice Provost at the University of Pittsburgh when a White, middle-aged book salesman came to my office. He stopped at my secretary's desk, she called me, and I had her send him into my office. The man suddenly stopped when he saw me and said, "Sorry, I'm looking for Professor Jack Daniel." Caught off guard, I said, "How may I help you" and he responded, "By helping me find Professor Jack Daniel" to which I answered, "I am Jack Daniel." With a reddened face, he turned and left.

Dissatisfied with the racial, cultural, and geographic isolation of CMU and motivated later by the assassination of Martin Luther King Jr., Jerri and I considered the possibility of my acquiring a position at one of the historically Black institutions. Seeking also an urban area where I could apply my new skills to resolving Black community problems and Jerri could work with urban public school children, I applied for and was offered a faculty position at Howard University. However, the Howard opportunity quickly fell apart.

In May, I received Howard employment papers with a section that required me to indicate my allegiance to the United States. I refused to do so because my new Black consciousness did not permit me to swear allegiance to my racist oppressor. My refusal got referred to a senior academic administrator and, during my meeting with him, he indicated that not only would I sign if I were to work there but also I would fare better at Howard if I were to cut my long hair and retire my dashikis in favor of business suits. I stood and left without saying a word. What could I possibly say to change the mind of a leading historically Black college senior administrator who, in my opinion, was so retrogressive in his thinking? To the extent that he was representative, Howard was not the place for me.

As I prepared to defend my dissertation in June of 1968, the Speech Department Chair, Jack Matthews, informed me that there were a number of pressing race-related issues at Pitt, and he believed I could be helpful should I be willing to return to Pitt and teach in the Department. He did not suggest that I might be helpful to the Department by doing something such as publishing the results of my research and, in turn, helping the Department gain a national scholarly reputation. Rather, his primary focus was with the possibility of me being a "utility" player to help with race-related problems on campus.

Not having a job, I quickly met with the Black student leaders who also urged me to return and help them. They saw themselves as having become more radical, and had changed their name from the Afro-American Cultural Society to the Black Action Society (BAS). Most importantly, during the coming academic year, they informed me of their intentions to make good on the action part of their name, and they would highly value my assistance in doing so. They too expressed no concern with my roles as a teacher and scholar.

After discussing with me their frustrations over their fruitless meetings with University administrators, the BAS Steering Committee members shared with me the following demands they had sent to Chancellor Wesley W. Posvar on May 30, 1968.

1. ...we demand that the Black Action Society be recognized immediately as the official representative body of the Black students on campus; thus, all affairs and programs affecting the Black Community on campus is first cleared with this body...

2. We demand that the University of Pittsburgh double its Black enrollment beginning September 1968 and to continue each year until the Black students compose at least 20% of the total population of the University... (This demand also included a Black recruiting team, Black oriented courses, an increase in Black faculty, a Black Studies program, and an Afro-American research center and support services to increase and maintain Black student enrollment.)

3. ...we demand that all negative labels, such as the aforementioned ("high risk" and "culturally deprived") be eliminated and that the impending orientation of the above students be coordinated with the Black Action Society.

4. ...we demand that all news releases and publicity affecting the Black community on campus be withheld until approved by the Black Action Society.

5. ...we demand that all programs that have been, are and will be instigated by the University, affecting Black students, be brought to the immediate attention of the Black Action Society.

6. ...that the number of Black faculty be increased... Also, that prospective Black professors be interviewed by the Black Action Society prior to hiring and that our opinion be one of the determining factors in the final decision of hiring.

7. ... That a Black Studies program, which would be staffed and directed by Black scholars in its entirety, be instituted immediately...

In addition to the foregoing, the 1968 document indicated,

Our concerns here go beyond these demands. It should be clearly understood to the University that we the Black Action Society are deeply committed to the current Black Revolution. We are not asking for white justice, but we will settle for nothing less than total justice by use of all means possible and required in order to achieve TRUE BLACK FREEDOM.

I was not only moved by the action-oriented BAS agenda and the Pitt administration's desire to get something done as compared to what I thought to be the "Negro status quo mind set" at Howard University, but I was also motivated by the extremely tumultuous race relations throughout the nation. Langston Hughes' poetic inquiry, "What happens to a dream deferred?" had been answered dramatically when Black anger exploded in a series of revolts. For example, more than 500 fires had been reported in Pittsburgh. Now, I had the proverbial "fire in the belly" which made me highly motivated to play a significant role in addressing race relations on campus.

As I increasingly did when making a difficult decision, I returned to the psychological refuge of my religious leaders' teachings. I recalled one of Reverend Johnson's favorite sermons, "Here am I. Send me!" After I read and re-read the following text (Isaiah 6: 6-9), I knew where I would be working in September 1968.

Then flew one of the seraphims unto me, having a live coal in his hands which he had taken with the tongs from the altar; And he laid it upon my mouth, and said, Lo, this hath touched thy lips; and thine iniquity is taken away, and thy sin purged. Also, I heard the voice of the Lord, saying, "Whom shall I send, and who will go for us" Then said I, Here am I; send me.

I thought I had morphed from a mis-educated, high school Negro to a full-fledged Black and proud man, ready to serve my people on the Pitt battlefield, but I had no idea how clueless I was regarding the nature of the battle I and other new Black faculty members would be fighting on historically White campuses.

By virtue of being recent recipients of doctoral degrees and in possession of large dosages of melanin, a number of young Black professionals were hired by White administrators to serve as their campus race experts. We were given reduced teaching loads in order that we might instead serve on various newly formed committees focused on addressing social matters. It mattered little that many new Black faculty had very little substantive professional expertise regarding the resolution of social issues or that some, like me, had as little as two semesters of full-time faculty experience. It seemed not to have occurred to them that there would be no long-term success in addressing the issues unless they were intimately involved, that they too had to help recruit Black students, that they too had to mentor Black students, that they too needed to modify the content of their courses to include Blacks as a focus of concern.

Desperate to avoid campus protests as well as related violence and, often with some genuine interest to address pressing problems, White administrators and senior faculty members expected their newly hired, Black junior faculty to recruit Black students, faculty, and administrators; mentor the enrolled Black students; attend meetings with contentious Blacks from the local community; and develop new courses focused on the "Black Experience." It was classic "crisis control" by "window dressing."

Simultaneously, we newly anointed race experts were ill-prepared when it came to understanding the factors that would weigh most heavily in faculty promotion decisions. We heard the repeated general statements regarding teaching, research and service, but did not know the true rank ordered importance of these factors was research, teaching, and service. We were naïve regarding the significance of things such as serving on faculty search committees; chairing a graduate program committee that not only made departmental admissions decisions but also determined who would receive fellowships; or serving as a member of the departmental executive committee that addressed budgetary and program priority matters; and participating in University-wide governance.

"Governance structures" seemed to be obstacles that racists threw in our way when we presented proposals for enhancing the Black presence on campus. After all, these "governance structures" were seldom used when we were hired or when the University committed new money to facilitate token Black enrollments.

Usually, it was not until the occasion of their promotion and tenure decisions that many Black faculty members realized that, for the most part, they were mere gadflies nipping, annoying, and in other ways agitating for change, but doing little to enhance their chances for academic promotion. Not only was publishing the administration's and senior faculty members' highest priority, but publishing in scholarly journals approved by one's respective professional discipline (Quarterly Journal of Speech) -not in new publications such as the Black Scholar or the Journal of Black Studies where many young Black faculty published.

We learned belatedly that we needed to teach core courses in our disciplines, in addition to designing and teaching new Black Studies courses. Our service to Black undergraduate students received praise, but we learned at the time of promotion decisions that tenure and promotion committee members valued much more highly the supervision of graduate students.

Given the discrepant expectations and related performances, many 1960s–1970s Black scholars amassed spectacular service records related to race matters, but failed to publish sufficiently in the appropriate scholarly journals. They primarily taught undergraduates instead of conducting graduate seminars, and left in disgust when they were denied promotion by their all-White senior faculty committee members. Liberal White faculty bemoaned the fact that the departing faculty members were "so good with 'those' students," "key to helping us enroll our one Black graduate student," and "we just don't know what we're going to do without them." Litigation against institutions was often rebuffed when administrators quickly pointed to the obscure but published departmental, school, and institutional guidelines for faculty promotion and tenure.

I too was so caught up "in the struggle" for my people that, at the time, it did not occur to me that I received no mentoring regarding my professional development. The possibility did not occur to me that the University administrators had no long-term interest in me as a scholar, that I was simply a short-term necessity to help address "social issues." Nor did it occur to me that "social issues" were not matters for which White faculty members would dirty their hands --that they were matters left to their newly hired "janitor."

To this day, Black faculty remain conflicted in terms of the time they spend helping to address campus matters related to Blacks and the time they devote to their teaching and scholarship. They remain conflicted in terms of teaching "mainstream" departmental courses as opposed to courses that focus on Blacks, e.g., to teach "The Rhetoric of Aristotle" or to teach the "Rhetoric of Black Americans." Similarly, there is the ongoing conflict associated with whether or not, at the time of a tenure and promotion decision, the senior White faculty will give equal weight to publications in a relatively new Journal of Black Studies that featured primarily Black scholars as compared to the long-term Quarterly Journal of Speech that had featured White scholars since the Speech Communication profession began.

When making a convention paper presentation, Black Speech Communication scholars, for example, still worry about whether their presentations will be viewed favorably by senior White faculty members if they participate in a program sponsored by the African American Communication and Culture Division, the Critical and Cultural Studies Division, or the Rhetorical and Communication Theory Division ---each with their significantly different racial group sponsorship.

Many Black faculty members assume the burden of being "twice as good" by demonstrating their competencies in the "traditional" areas of their respective disciplines as represented by their senior White colleagues and, at the same time, participating in matters of concern to their Black professional caucus. Still others seek refuge in the contemporary Africana Studies departments where they are rewarded for teaching and research related to the African diaspora. Some refuse to embrace the historically White campus struggle and either take positions at historically Black institutions or leave academia.

CHAPTER ELEVEN:

Negotiating Demands

Just as Br'er Rabbit struggled and became increasingly entangled with the tar baby, fighting for race-related changes caused me to become increasingly bound to Pitt. My entanglements solidified when I accepted an invitation from the Black Action Society (BAS) student leaders to participate in their weekly Steering Committee meetings. As the only faculty member who met regularly with them, I emerged as the Black faculty spokesperson on behalf of the BAS.

Daily, I increasingly became aware of the fact that I dwelled in two worlds. One was populated by radical Black undergraduates dedicated to rediscovering and glorifying their ancient African past, affecting immediate changes on campus, and providing services to the local Black community. My other world consisted of White faculty and administrators who were angered by the BAS' confrontational tactics and staunchly committed to their core enterprises steeped in European intellectual traditions. Even for the liberal Whites, gradualism was their preferred style for making changes as opposed to the radical pace proposed by the BAS.

Tension rapidly mounted for me as I shuttled between my communities of conflicting expectations. The BAS wanted Black faculty members hired immediately to teach courses related to the yet to be defined Black experience. White administrators asked me, a novice holder of a doctorate, where they could find "highly qualified" faculty given the small pool of Blacks with doctorates.

The BAS vociferously demanded more than 150 Black freshmen admitted for the 1969 fall term. The administration argued that it was impossible to do so given the woefully inadequate job the public schools were doing to produce college qualified Blacks. The BAS declared that it spoke for the entire Black community, but senior administrators insisted they were just a student organization, albeit that I and a community representative served on their Steering Committee. Both sides clamored for the other to understand them.

Hovering in the middle of two antagonistic campus communities, I strongly advocated for the students' demands, but also encouraged them to appreciate the fact that the University was bound to abide by its often time consuming governance rules and procedures. Simultaneously, I urged the administration and faculty to consider the long legacy of slavery, the terrible atrocities of racism, the harm being done to children in segregated schools and, therefore, the need for them to respond in a positive and timely fashion to the students' demands lest we too experience the campus violence rapidly spreading across the nation.

A late October 1968, BAS Steering Committee meeting ended when the students concluded that the time had come for the BAS to make good on its stated commitment to "use all means possible and required in order to achieve TRUE BLACK FREEDOM." Heretofore, a number of factors such as fear of police brutality and/ or being expelled contributed partially to the students not acting precipitously. Most of the leaders were first generation college students for whom families had made many sacrifices in hopes that their children would have a better life as a result of earning their degrees. Expulsion from Pitt would have been disastrous for these students and their families, and the possibility of being jailed was even worse.

Some, including me, still hoped that a less confrontational approach would yield results. Through private meetings with Chancellor Wesley Posvar, I tried in vain to get him and others to respond affirmatively to some of the students' specific demands. My frustration grew as I often heard what the students had previously heard from Chancellor Posvar and other senior administrators, e.g.,

"But where are we going to find that many qualified Black students, faculty or administrators? How would we pay for all of that even if it were possible?"

The BAS leaders and I countered with claims that the University officials held racist definitions of what it meant to be a qualified student, that they were being elitist with their focus on standardized test scores, grades, and high school class ranks. We urged them to also consider factors such as participation in church choirs, leadership in community organizations, achievements in the arts, and, indeed, having literally survived a poverty and crime infested neighborhood as supplemental evidence of a Black students' qualifications.

Regarding standardized test scores and other quantitative measures, we made the case that lower Black scores were in part a function of racially biased tests and, in general, not having an equal educational opportunity to do well on such tests. I offered as evidence of culturally biased test questions such as the following: "_____ Washington was the first President of _____. At that time, no White administrator answered that "Booker T." was the first president of "Tuskegee Institute."

Since there were no examples of established Black Studies programs, some White administrators engaged in protracted struggle by repeatedly asking rhetorically, "What exactly is Black Studies?" The BAS leaders cited the works of the distinguished scholars W.E. B. Dubois, E. Franklin Frazier, and Carter G. Woodson as examples of Black Studies research. I often pointed to the study of African languages as well as Black Americans' rhetoric, citing scholarly works as fast as I had time to discover and read them. For proposed literature courses, we listed the contemporary works of Leroy Jones, Sonia Sanchez, Don L. Lee as well as writers from the Harlem Renaissance.

We wanted the University administrators to accept in principle the idea of Black Studies as an academic discipline by creating a department and, in turn, beginning the pursuit of staffing. The University administrators protracted the matter by making use of the fact that there was a dearth of Black holders of doctorates in all disciplines and, hence, repeatedly stalled by asking, "But where can we find a qualified professor to teach such courses?"

As the Fall term ended with no specific positive responses having been made to the BAS' demands, the students were pushed closer to the precipice of direct and dangerous actions. The Steering Committee decided to focus on taking their final examinations and, after the Christmas break, try one final meeting with the Chancellor. On the morning of January 15, 1969, buttressed by the rhythms of African drums, about 25 Black students and I marched to the Chancellor's office, and forced our way into the reception area. Our drummers played very loudly for about ten minutes, commemorating our African roots and celebrating Martin Luther King Jr.'s birthday. When the Chancellor's personal secretary arrived, we demanded to see the Chancellor. He appeared about fifteen minutes later, indicated he would not meet under duress, and told us to schedule an appointment.

The students immediately left in anger, mumbling profanity. Before departing, I cautioned the Chancellor that the students were likely to take more desperate actions. The Chancellor advised me to do my best to get the students to avoid such actions, to schedule an appointment, and let them know that bursting into his office was inappropriate. His assistant warned me, "And don't you, Jack Daniel, ever come back here and threaten the Chancellor." Little did I know, at the time, that the University was prepared to make good on the threat by having hired a local law firm to possibly file charges against me and others.

Years later, I obtained a copy of a legal document in which I and others were specifically named as defendants for having "...conspired and agreed to and are staging a sit-in, rally, demonstration and protests... They have unlawfully and continue unlawfully to prevent the Chancellor and other officers of the plaintiff from conducting normal University business..." Two such Complaints were drafted and sent to one of the Chancellor's top assistants, with an offer to "tailor one or the other of the Complaints to the actual situation." Fortunately, they were never used.

Walking to my office, I fumed, "Schedule another damn appointment! Can you believe that, after all of this time, he wants another goddamn appointment! There is no way in hell that I'm going to tell the students to do that. And that jerk had the nerve to threaten me! Well, we'll see."

Later that evening while I was teaching, approximately seventy students sprung their carefully planned surprise by taking over the University's $8 million Computer Center which was located in the Cathedral of Learning and processed faculty members' research data, institutional financial records, student records, and most of the critical institutional management data. After chaining the doors to the room and disabling access to elevators, the students telephoned the Chancellor's office and indicated they would not leave until their demands were met. There was also innuendo regarding the possible destruction of the computer technology.

At approximately 8:30 p.m., with my adrenalin at possibly an all-time high, I proceeded to the Chancellor's office. Police officers and the President of the Faculty Senate escorted me to the room where several senior administrators had assembled. Subsequently, two other Blacks made up our negotiating team: Assistant to the Provost, Eugene Davis and Assistant Dean of Students, Luddy Hayden. On behalf of the BAS, a student Lora R. Head Davis Hubbard took notes. The Chancellor arrived shortly thereafter and negotiations began.

In accordance with previous plans, those of us representing the BAS indicated that, prior to discussing the demands, the students in the Computer Center had to be given the food and blankets provided by community members. To my surprise, the Chancellor agreed, and I was even more surprised when he agreed to our demand that no legal actions be taken against anyone in the Computer Center provided they did not destroy University property. Our third starting point was that the demands had to be taken up in the order written, and that we would not move to the next demand until the previous one had been addressed to the satisfaction of all parties. As some of his White staff members sat with sullen red faces, the Chancellor also agreed to this procedure.

Next, we wrangled over details such as what it meant for the students to leave the Computer Center in a "prompt and peaceful" manner. After debating the specifics of those terms, we tried to advance specific numbers of Black faculty and administrators to be appointed during a specified time period, but the Chancellor preferred to write in more general terms. As hours passed, I became increasingly anxious about what might happen if negotiations failed and the students were confronted by armed police. Everyone was very relieved when the Chancellor signed an agreement which was shared with those inside the Computer Center, and the students peacefully left the Computer Center.

The agreement read as follows:

The following is agreed between the University of Pittsburgh and the Black Action Society.

1. *There will be no punitive measures taken by the University against persons in the computer room provided that it is vacated promptly, peacefully and without damage.*

2. *The University will appoint an officer and a recruiting team to recruit black students, and they will be appointed as soon as members of the Black Action Society can locate such personnel, screen them and recommend their appointment to the University.*

3. *The University will recruit additional black faculty, administrators and other personnel at all levels:*

4. *The Chancellor will arrange for meetings between members of the Black Action Society and department heads of the University concerning such recruitment.*

5. *Members of the Black Action Society will study the University's structure to determine where black administrators, faculty and other personnel are needed and will recommend to the University where such personnel should be placed.*

6. *Space will be provided in Hillman Library where there will be books, periodicals and other materials to the extent that a person*

who wanted to write a doctoral thesis on a topic related to Afro-Americans will find materials available in sufficient quantity.

7. *The Chancellor will urge the faculty to establish an institute for black studies for research and teaching, with a director and assistant director to be appointed by June, and that these people, when they arrive, will have the necessary funds available for their work.*

8. *The Chancellor will recommend to the University Senate that black members of the University community including students, faculty, administrators and staff be excused from their duties on February 21 {Note: The BAS wanted the day of Malcolm X's assassination to be a University holiday.} without penalty; it also will be recommended to the University Senate that January 15, the birthday of the late Rev. Martin Luther King, Jr. will be made a University holiday.*

Without unnecessary delay, the Chancellor will address himself to the other issues in the original demands made by the Black Action Society on May 20, 1968.

Immediately after the take-over, the students were emboldened by the notion that they were confirmed combat veterans, true militants, angry Black men and women willing to act by any means necessary. They had been baptized in battle and rewarded for their actions. They had confirmation of Frederick Douglass' dictum that power concedes nothing without a demand. Stokely Carmichael was right when he said Blacks had to quit begging and take what belongs to them. They, like Black student groups and a few Black faculty at Cornell, UCLA, Rutgers, and others across the country, had realized significant gains only when they engaged in activities that posed threats to people and property.

As demonstrated over time, the Computer Center take-over participants created the historical moment that future BAS leadership would deem the most important, revolutionary, liberation moment in Black history at Pitt. Indeed, every institutionalized Black-related effort at Pitt through the first decade and a half of the twenty-first century emerged from the agreements reached that early 1969 morning, e.g., academic support service programs for Black students; scholarship support for diversity purposes; the Africana Studies Department; the African American Library Collection; and a significant ongoing cohort of Black faculty, staff and administrators, including Donald M. Henderson, who eventually became Provost.

Notwithstanding the successful outcomes, I privately agonized about how close the involved students, with my and others' involvement, had moved to a point of potential violence. I thought about the hurt that might have been felt by the parents and relatives if there had been arrests, convictions, disruption of college careers or, still worse, the loss of young lives.

I wanted more of my people rightfully participating in the life of the University, but I had never been prepared to risk limb, life, or career to realize those goals. Although I was very pleased to have taken part in the negotiation of the BAS' demands with the administration, I felt considerable guilt for not having experienced the personal risk of being in the Computer Center. Recognizing that I was not prepared to achieve true outlaw status and not wanting to be hypocritical, I vowed to never again to participate in a Computer Center type event unless I too was in the direct line of action, to never again depend on Black students as the primary "battering ram" for change.

In order to make greater progress in addressing race-related matters on historically White campuses, the White campus community must come to grips with the fact that White racism continues to exist in epidemic proportions on as well as off-campus. It was not a matter of "youthful transgressions" when the following took place in 2018:

- Cal Polytechnic (White fraternity members in blackface)
- DePauw (racial threats posted in bathroom)
- Lehigh (racial graffiti)
- Pitt (racist social media post)
- Southern California (racist flyer)
- Syracuse (racist fraternity initiation video)
- University of Alabama (racist video posted)

- University of Oregon (racist remarks on sidewalk) and
- Yale (White Yale student calls police after observing a Black Yale student sleeping in the dormitory lounge)

When it comes to a "most livable city" such as Pittsburgh, Pitt constituents must heed the June 26, 2018, words of Allegheny County Controller Chelsa Wagner:

> We must all confront the deep and ugly disparities of race and privilege in this region; disparities that run deeper and are more insidious than nearly anywhere else in our country. We must engage in a conversation that is and has always been woefully lacking in Pittsburgh, and commit meaningfully to both urgent and sustained action.

> That begins, I believe, by admitting unequivocally that we live what is best referred to as a "tale of two cities." The reality of daily life for those who are White (like me) is drastically different from the reality of daily life for people of color in this region. ...For Black people in Pittsburgh, the designation of "Most Livable City" has never included them...

To insure that Pitt is not a "tale of two cities," the current University leadership should take steps to insure that Pitt offers, to all if its constituents, the "world of possibilities" which Chancellor Emeritus Mark A. Nordenberg discussed in 2102

> Exceeding our record-setting $2 billion campaign goal is a momentous milestone made possible by the extraordinary generosity of University supporters, who have demonstrated their commitment to Pitt and its long-standing mission of building better lives through the power of education and research ...More important than that extraordinarily large dollar amount is the impact that these funds will have—on the lives of our hard-working and high-achieving students, on the ambitious and often trailblazing work of our world-class faculty, and on the economic strength and vibrancy of our home region...

(Pitt News Services, October 12, 2012).

Now is the time for a similar concerted effort to enable Black students, faculty, staff and administrators to participate equally in all that Pitt offers. To do this, we must go beyond Black students serving as the advance guard for social change. Nor is the best path to success a matter of shifting the burden primarily to Black faculty, staff and administrators.

The current situation at Pitt is truly one for which the entire village is needed. As such, the societal demands now placed on Pitt are as follows:

Diversity and Inclusion. To enable the University becoming a "world-class model of diversity and inclusion," the University leadership should consult appropriately and then

1. promulgate the categories of collective human differences (diversity) that constitute the University's top five institutional priorities;

2. state the specific goals each University responsibility center has for fulfilling the University's top five diversity priorities;

3. declare the acceptable means of measuring the specified top five diversity outcomes;

4. determine appropriate diversity benchmark institutions and do the comparisons; and

5. produce an annual University report on diversity outcomes.

Blacks as a High Institutional Diversity Priority. Black students, staff, faculty and administrators should be declared one of the University's highest diversity priorities given [1] the Federal mandate to desegregate the Commonwealth of Pennsylvania's state-owned institutions of higher education; [2] Pennsylvania's programmatic efforts to support economically and educationally disadvantaged students; [3] the racial composition of the population served by the University of Pittsburgh; [4] the historical underrepresentation of Blacks, at the University of Pittsburgh in particular as well as in higher education in general; and [5] the continued racial gaps in educational achievement, wealth, health and most measures of wellbeing.

Blacks and Inclusion. The University must provide operational definitions for what is meant by the practice of inclusion, e.g., state the specific steps to be taken in order to make effective use of human differences to improve classroom learning, administrative decision making, staff performance, and shared governance. The University should fund demonstration projects whereby specific aspects of inclusion such as race improve the quality of the University's administration, faculty, staff, and students.

While the foregoing recommendations are addressed to Pitt, it is deemed that they are applicable to many other historically White institutions.

CHAPTER TWELVE:

Building Black Studies

January 1969 through July 1973 was the fastest paced, most intense, nerve racking period of my life. The emotional turmoil was brewed in the context of [1] an embattled Black student body and White administration as well as [2] the difficulties associated with implementing a new academic program that was a radical departure from institutional norms in terms of substance, staffing, and students. The proximate beginning was when, within a month of having successfully negotiated their demands, the newly empowered Black Action Society (BAS) persuaded Dean Dave Halliday to send me the following February 18, 1969 letter.

Dear Jack:

I am pleased to accept the recommendation of the Black Action Society that you be appointed Director of Black Studies... I am strongly in favor of a Department of Black Studies which would have the same autonomy as the Department of Music, the Department of Chemistry, the Department of Political Science... The Department would be provided with a budget and would be autonomous in the control of the requirements for a degree (undergraduate or graduate) in Black Studies... The proposed department does not as yet exist and must be sanctioned by the Faculty of Arts and Sciences Council and, perhaps the general faculty... Your present position is somewhat nebulous but, in two months' time, I am sure that we can define it to our mutual satisfaction. Your title as "director" may be changed to "chairman," depending on the outcome of wishes of the Faculty. We are agreed that White students may take courses in Black Studies... I will meet with the BAS as often as they wish (in the evening if that is more convenient for them) to make sure that the lines of communication are kept open...

I was reluctant to accept the position largely because I had already begun playing a lead role in advocating for my professional Association to be more responsive to Blacks, Hispanics, women, and contemporary social issues. After chairing the Speech Association of America's (SAA) December 1968 special ad hoc Committee on Social Relevance and, subsequently meeting with approximately one dozen Black professionals, I emerged as the Chair of the newly formed SAA Black Caucus.

Foremost on the Black Caucus' agenda were the following time-consuming action items: the formulation of strategies for recruiting more Black doctoral students; implementing convention programs related to Black Communication; realizing greater participation by Black Americans in the business of the SAA; and developing a national research and teaching agenda related to Black Communication.

At Pitt, I had designed and begun to teach two new courses, i.e., "Black Rhetoric" and "Black People and the Mass Media." In addition, I was editing a book on Black Communication teaching and research. As such, I viewed myself as an emerging Black Communication scholar as opposed to a yet to be defined Black Studies scholar. An additional source of ambivalence emanated from the fact that I was not in complete agreement with the BAS' Black Studies aspirations.

Although I had worked with the students in presenting their demands, my expectation was that the programmatic implementation of Black Studies would be led by some academic leader for whom the University would conduct a national search. In addition, I did not believe undergraduate students and/or their community supporters had sufficient expertise to play vital roles in defining and developing an academic discipline. In particular, I disagreed with the students regarding who constituted qualified faculty.

In accordance with standard University policies, I held that new faculty members should hold earned doctorates or, at a minimum, be in the process of completing their dissertations. The students' disposition was made quite clear to me during a BAS Steering Committee meeting when one student argued absurdly that pimps, prostitutes, and welfare recipients knew as much about the "economics of the ghetto" as any Ph.D. After he seriously suggested the name of a local militant high school graduate to teach such a course, the Steering Committee unanimously endorsed the recommendation that I interview the person.

Seeking to appease the group, I interviewed the person but did not hire him after he agreed that he was not qualified to teach the course. Still, the students were adamant in arguing that the earned doctorate was not a necessity and, moreover, they were not interested in "intellectual bullshit" published in the "so-called scholarly journals." Rather, they had a greater interest in faculty members who taught and provided services to the Black communities on and off-campus.

Another hotly contested point between the BAS, me, and the University administration had to do with whether Black Studies faculty members should hold joint appointments in Black Studies and another existing academic department. The prevailing view within the BAS was that only Black faculty members "hung up on associating with the White disciplines" wanted to remain in the racist departments from which they received their doctorates. Truly revolutionary brothers and sisters would break the intellectual chains their old departments held on their brains by holding appointments only in Black Studies. Their "legitimacy" need not be confirmed by one of the "traditional" departments.

The students' perception of my "Blackness" was put on the line when the students urged me to give up my faculty appointment in the Speech Department and I refused to do so. It made no sense to me to not have faculty status as I worked to develop a Black Studies Department and, as a compromise, the BAS agreed that I could remain in the Speech Department until Black Studies became a department as opposed to a program.

While I stewed about assuming the position of Director, what surprised me the most was the extent to which the students and some community activists believed the Directorship to be a major professional opportunity for me or, as one student stated, "a new big-time job." As opposed to finding myself presented with an attractive career change, it seemed to me that circumstances, partially of my own making, were forcing me to accept a highly problematic position. Moreover, they had no idea regarding the extent to which other institutions were pursuing me to leave Pitt and join their Speech Communication departments and/or become a member of their administrations as some form of "special assistant for minority affairs." I was tempted to explore some of the many invitations for campus visits, but I was too mired in Pitt circumstances to give them serious consideration.

During a long discussion with my wife, it was her sense that taking the position was something I should do if, in the final analysis, I truly believed in the importance of developing Black Studies as an academic discipline. In the end, I felt obligated to accept the Director position largely because there was no one else on the campus to do so, the University was not committed to conducting a national search, and I could not have sustained my posture as a revolutionary Black campus leader if I opted not to take the position.

My private intent was to serve long enough to design the Black Studies curriculum and other key programmatic aspects, hire key staff including my replacement, then return to the Speech Department, and put most of my service energy into the work of the SAA Black Caucus. I hoped to leave Black Studies by the end of the coming August, having hired faculty to teach the first cohort of students. However, it only took a month of internecine conflicts for me to offer the BAS my resignation from Black Studies.

What should have come as no surprise to me was the Steering Committee's non-compromising position that it was the final authority on all Black Studies resource matters. They reasoned that their actions had led to the Chancellor's concessions, the

Chancellor and the Dean were dealing directly with them, and I would do the same.

The Black students and I continued to argue about Black Studies decision making, and unable to sway a single opinion, during an early March Saturday morning, I offered my resignation to the students. That night, one of my key opponents called to indicate that some "brothers" would like to discuss some "Black business" with me. Naively, I invited them to my apartment. When they arrived, once again I heard allegations of me having become a counter-revolutionary. When all were seated, their spokesperson began with, "You know man, you're either part of the problem or part of the solution. You were cool from the jump, but you've gone off into this thing, acting like the White folks who run Pitt. I mean, like, you've gone real counter, man!"

Before I could respond, a student known for his karate expertise added, "Yeah, we tried to discuss this with you, but just like one of those White boys you're patterning yourself after, you grabbed your coat and split. And talking trash as you left didn't help." Another student added, "That's right. I mean, in a matter of days, you've tried to betray us by insisting on an old, elitist, European method of administration, with you at the top making decisions on your own."

Knowing it was useless to say anything to my "brothers," I simply listened. Eventually, I agreed to attend one more meeting with the BAS Steering Committee to resolve our differences. A few days after that several hour meeting, I agreed that the BAS, not me or the University, would make final decisions regarding Black Studies.

During the ensuing days, I concurred that the BAS would hire Curtiss E. Porter to serve as the Associate Director, albeit that I had to make the recommendation to the University and get their approval. Porter was a key founding member of the BAS, had extensive local community connections, and was enrolled as a Pitt graduate student. He was the campus leader at the forefront of raising consciousness, e.g., identifying connections between Blacks and Africans, bringing Black political speakers to campus, and promoting local Black artists. Indeed, he best wore the mantle of campus activist and contributed significantly to the articulation and implementation of the Black Studies plan for Pitt.

The remainder of March through early May was taken up with obtaining a permanent operating budget, hiring support staff, identifying a few courses and faculty for the fall, writing a long-term proposal for Black Studies, and securing offices which we painted red, black and green, the colors we associated with Black cultural nationalism. Incense burned constantly. The sounds of John Coltrane and Pharaoh Saunders added to what we deemed an appropriate Black revolutionary ambience on the 11*th* floor of Pitt's Cathedral of Learning.

Much of our administrative attention was subsequently directed to the biggest disagreement with the University administration, i.e., whether we would have a set of courses to be taught in existing departments, a set of courses in a new Black Studies Department with only undergraduate courses, or a new Black Studies Department with undergraduate and graduate curricula. Most of the University's existing senior administrators and faculty wanted us to start small by having only courses in select departments. They allegedly feared the creation of an isolated program with only Black students and faculty. They also argued that White students too could benefit from the courses and they would be more likely to enroll if the courses were cross listed with "established," "well-respected" programs. Their sentiments were echoed by a few local community Black professionals who urged the University not to create a "ghetto department" serving only Blacks. I, Associate Director Porter, and the BAS Steering Committee members steadfastly held to the necessity of an independent academic department as a minimal University commitment.

A few vocal White faculty members proclaimed that there was no such thing as a Black Studies discipline. We countered that the only reason it was not a recognized academic discipline was because racist Eurocentric professors believed everything worthy of study emanated from Europeans. Such faculty members, for example, denied the African origins of civilization and held that Egypt was not part of Africa! Eventually, the formal proposal that Associate

Director Porter and I submitted led to an escalation of these and related tensions.

The document, *"The Black Paper for Black Studies,"* went much further than anyone anticipated. As one might expect, key administrators and faculty members were aghast when they read the opening lines of our treatise:

> *As Black agents of change and overthrow, we will find it necessary to study the history of the imperialist, the colonialist, the capitalist entrepreneur, the management middle class, and other agents of the White status quo in order to find out where they are coming from with their interminable meetings, sessions, counter-sessions, dialogue, etc. We have to do this in order to correct the image that we as colonial subjects have of the White "manager-possessors"...*

Much to the central administration's chagrin, we proposed a School of Black Studies that included the following: Division of Black Political, Social and Economic Science; the Division of Natural Science Health Professions; Division of the Black Studies Research Institute; Division of Culture and Black Art; a Black Community Institute, and a Floating Black University. Each Division would have multiple Departments. We indicated that the School of Black Studies should report to a new employee with the title of Vice Chancellor of Afro-American Affairs.

In response to our proposal, Acting Dean Steel Gow's May 26, 1969 letter committed a budget of $105,000 for the 1969-70 academic year. He explicitly denied approval of the School of Black Studies and noted that half of all faculty appointments had to be joint appointments with other departments. After caucusing, Porter, I and the BAS Steering Committee members indicated our rejection of Gow's terms by first refusing to respond to his letter and, secondly, not honoring his written requests to meet with him. When I saw him on campus, I refused to speak.

Instead of meeting with Acting Dean Gow, we requested a meeting with Provost Charles Peake and Chancellor Posvar, both of whom insisted that the Dean also had to attend. We agreed to the Dean attending but, in turn, we insisted that two members of the BAS' Political Action Force had to attend. After several meetings, Chancellor Posvar sent me a June 20, 1969 letter in which he supported the establishment of an interdisciplinary Department of Black Studies. He did not approve a School of Black Studies and noted that the "Black Paper for Black Studies" was "...more in the nature of a political manifesto than an academic proposal."

Porter and I knew it was not possible to immediately implement a School of Black Studies absent qualified faculty members. Most importantly, while normal faculty searches took place throughout the academic year, we had only the rest of June and July to search for faculty, hire them and get courses listed for September. Hence, we accepted the departmental status with two caveats.

First, we made it known to the Chancellor that we would not abandon the concept of a School of Black Studies. Second, we would not use the name Black Studies for what we deemed to be merely the first department. Instead, the unit would be known as the Department of Black Community, Education, Research and Development (DBCERD). The DBCERD name took us beyond the bounds of a traditional academic department by emphasizing a community-based component.

Although our primary community education project took the form of a child care center that was supported by an external grant, there were those inside and outside the University who viewed our notion of a "community institute" as a front for organizing militant Black community forces. On many occasions when I met with University administrators, I often received their nervous cautions regarding the need to stick to our primary on-campus academic mission. They had no idea of just how much that too was my preference given my many community-based conflicts.

My life was constantly threatened by radicals who had concerns with my "Blackness" and/or the "non-revolutionary" nature of my conduct. One very hot, muggy Friday night in July, I arrived at my apartment building around 11 p.m. A neighbor invited me to join a party that was in progress. After I entered his apartment and sat on the sofa, an obviously drug-induced high person stuck a pistol in my side and asked, "Why are you fucking up Black Studies?" A friend of his handed me a bottle of wine and, when I detected the presence of something in addition to wine in the bottle, I took only a small sip. That led to, "So, the brother doesn't even want to drink with us Niggers anymore!"

Angry with the guy who had duped me and unwilling to drink further from the bottle just to identify as a "brother," I asked sarcastically, "So, a brother has to get high to be a brother?" One older, bearded, near drunk, by day community activist answered, "See, motherfucker, that's why we bees needin' to deal with intellectual motherfuckers like you."

Now thoroughly disgusted but sensing unknown trouble if I tried to leave, I said, "So talk to me so that I can get the hell out of here." The supposed revolutionary brothers passed a joint around as they forcefully asked questions such as "So, why can't you spend a little of that University money in the community?" "What's this shit about only Negroes with doctorates can work in the program?" "Why don't you spend more time in the community with the folks who made them give you your gig?" Never once was I permitted to answer any of the questions. When the joint got to me and I passed it on without putting it to my lips, the brother with the pistol first snorted some cocaine and then asked with a smirk, "Should I shoot this jive ass motherfucker?"

Fearful that he might accidentally shoot me or do so if encouraged by others, I said, "This situation reminds me of what happened in the early part of Richard Wrights' <u>Black Boy</u>. Those guys could rob Black people, but when it came to robbing an old nearly blind White man, they couldn't follow through. So, now, none of you have shot a White man, but you're ready to shoot me." Fortunately for me, the duplicitous guy followed up with, "Come on now, Jack. We're all brothers and nobody is going to shoot anybody. El Malik, put the gun away and let's talk to the brother."

Their biggest disagreement with me related to my refusal to use departmental funds to support some of their protest activities. One case in point was my refusal to provide airfare for several of them to fly to Detroit and participate in an event related to the founding of the Republic of New Africa. After about an hour of their being too high to make sense to themselves much less me, I received the warning, "We'll be watching you, Nigger!" Then a red-eyed head-nodding brother added, "Until you get yourself together, our Nation (a local community group) is severing diplomatic relationships with you. Now get your ass on out of here."

I didn't wait for a second opportunity to leave. Fighting with White faculty members and administrators was very frustrating, but it hurt deeply that it was from Blacks that I received the most grief. Moses' disappointment with his people as he led them out of Egypt came to mind and I wondered what sins I had committed that would prevent me from seeing the promised land of Black Studies scholarship and teaching. I said nothing to campus administrators about being confronted because I was too ashamed to let White University officials know about these Black on Black matters. At the time, I didn't realize just how much I might have been a pawn who shielded White administrators from some Blacks' justifiable anger.

After talking with my wife, we decided to seek a bit of refuge with an August vacation at her parent's home in Sacramento. Before leaving for California, I visited a doctor to check my sense of constantly needing to urinate but was unable to do so when I tried. As soon as the doctor saw me, he asked me to look into a mirror and tell him what I saw. Not noticing anything out of the ordinary, he asked me to look at my dry lips which he said was a sign of tension. Then he added, "Some of us have been noticing what all you are doing at that University and we are worried for you. You seem headed for a nervous breakdown. You need to get away from it all." After concluding his examination, I was quite embarrassed when he provided medicine to calm my nerves. It just could not be that the macho man I perceived myself to be was having "mental" problems, something I thought to be the province of "crazy White people."

That afternoon, I took a dose of the medicine and I experienced no effect. When I remained stressed, despite having taken a second evening dose, I decided not to take more of the medicine. Two days later, before boarding the airplane that stopped in Chicago before proceeding to Sacramento, I gave the medicine another chance. To my surprise, after the plane was airborne I went into a very deep and enjoyable one hour sleep. I woke up when Jerri shook me and I noticed that nearly all of the other passengers had gotten off the airplane. After my connecting flight departed for Sacramento, I ate a snack, took another pill, and slept for three hours.

Once relaxed and far away from Black Studies, the pills proved to be so powerful that I was unable to function during the day if I took them as prescribed. After not taking any for two days in Sacramento, my urinary symptoms disappeared and I could not recall the last time I had been so relaxed. More than that, I realized how little attention I had given to my month-old daughter, Marijata.

I had forgotten how happy we were when Jerri found out she was pregnant, just weeks before we had scheduled medical appointments for the purpose of assessing why we had tried but failed over the past year. We discussed a variety of names throughout her pregnancy and, when our daughter was born, agreed on Marijata which resulted from the joining of Mari and Jata, the name of a great ancient West African ruler also known as Sundiata. We especially liked the aspect of the name referring to liberator and the fact that under Mari Jata's rule, the foundation was laid for a prosperous Mali Empire. It was only now, away from the Black Studies grind, that I began to think deeply about contributing to my daughter's healthy growth and development.

Shaken by the realization of the emotional toll my administrative experience was taking on me as well as my relationships with my family, I knew that my Black Studies days were numbered, notwithstanding the surprising content of a letter that I received from Chancellor Posvar while I was in Sacramento --a letter that indicated I was promoted to Associate Professor, with tenure as well as a title change to Chairman instead of Director.

After a much needed four-week rest, I returned to Pittsburgh and participated in an increasingly bitter internecine struggle within the Department. For the 1970–71 and 1971–72 academic years, the Department had 11 and 15 full-time faculty, respectively. One result of this rapid hiring was a curriculum that reflected more of a smorgasbord of introductory courses rather than a curriculum emanating from a curriculum philosophy along with goals, objectives, and a set of courses providing intellectual depth. Attempts to articulate the Department's major brought forth never ending disagreements regarding what should be the required upper level courses. Our curriculum meetings inevitably bogged down when arguments for specific required courses were clearly based on ideological and personal differences among the faculty and, at times, the curriculum disputes evolved into personal attacks.

Within the Department, battle lines were drawn between those who maintained that scholarly publications were essential and those who refused to engage in the scholarly publication enterprise. Still others maintained that publications in Black newspapers, magazines, and emerging journals such as the <u>Black Scholar</u> and the <u>Western Journal of Black Studies</u> were more appropriate than publications in the journals associated with the established Arts and Sciences disciplines. The latter point, in turn, renewed the arguments regarding those who had joint appointments with Black Studies and other departments. Those with joint appointments were perceived to be less committed to Black Studies and cooperating with the administration's ultimate goal of dismantling the Department and, instead, offering an array of courses in other departments.

Another critically important factor regarding the majority of the initial hires was the fact that only three held doctoral degrees and, as such, were trained to conduct research currently recognized by the University for faculty promotion. Several members did not publish sufficiently because they were pursuing graduate degrees as they worked full-time. The net result of not publishing was that many of the original hires never received permanent employment at the University. With each denial of tenure came a round of volatile student, faculty, and community protests.

The unending internal Departmental conflicts eventually wore me down, and the birth of my son, Omari, in October 1971, gave me a final reason to terminate my relationship with the Department. With two young children, I was not about to leave Jerri functioning as a single parent if somehow I became a victim, of all things, of some terrible Black on Black crime. Nor was I prepared for my mental health to deteriorate to a point that would prevent me from functioning well as a husband and father.

After months of privately rationalizing my decision, I finally sent a September 6, 1972 letter of resignation to the faculty, the BAS Chair, and the University administration. My resignation ushered in an array of internal disagreements regarding the future governance of the Department. Unable to resolve our many differences, some members secretly met with the heretofore bad White Dean and other administrators. That led to accusations of those faculty members being traitors to the Black struggle, and our meetings became increasingly ugly as personal slurs were hurled.

Late in the academic year, a stunning blow came to me when several of the faculty members wrote a formal statement accusing me of having "impugned the integrity of the Department." The complaints were submitted to the administration, and since the Dean was out of the country, the Provost decided that the Black Vice Provost, Dr. Donald M. Henderson, would hear the charges against me.

In his April 16, 1973 memorandum to the faculty, Provost Rhoten A. Smith wrote:

> I have been informed that the above noted faculty meeting (Friday April 20, 1973) has been scheduled to review the substance of charges against Dr. Jack L. Daniel, the Chairman of your department. I am further informed that these charges question the integrity and honesty with which Dr. Daniel has conducted at least some of the affairs of the department. As you know such charges are matters of very serious import and warrant careful and scrupulous consideration.

Instead of meeting with Vice Provost Henderson, faculty members and I opted to meet by ourselves at which time I would hear and respond to the charges. On May 9, 1973, we held an eight-hour meeting at which time we argued vociferously. Tempers flared! Threats and counter threats were made against each other! Some walked out of the meeting, and the meeting ended without a motion to adjourn. Nothing more came of the charges given that my term of office ended the last day of June, and, much more importantly, all attention turned to my successor.

With an 11-4 vote, the Department opted for Porter to serve as the acting Chair of the Department, and I forwarded that vote to Dean Jerome L. Rosenberg and the BAS. Dean Rosenberg rejected the faculty's vote and, in a June 15, 1973 memorandum to the faculty, stated, "I have appointed Professor Fela Sowande to be Acting Chairman of the Department of Black Studies effective July1, 1973." That night, a "Black Dispatch" addressed to "The Black Community" was circulated on campus and throughout the local community.

The "Black Dispatch" included the following:

> *The University of Pittsburgh with sanction of its nigga overseer... is in the process of an extensive re-organization of its plantation. Its first move was the unjustifiable dismissal of ..., but more recent is the move on the Black Studies Department, which just happens to be the national model of similar programs.*

> *The sliminess surfaced when Jack Daniel resigned as Chairman. The Black Studies faculty twice voted in Curtiss Porter as acting chairman until a permanent chairman was found. A group of unhappy house nigga's ... went crying to Dean Rosenberg about the decision. Dean Rosenberg, behind the shield of running dog lackeys toppled the decision of the Black Studies Department and appointed Chief Fela Sowande, (who resides in the cosmos of the occult),... Of course, Massa Rosenberg would not have made such a move without the consent of ... who is a snitch that sits on top of most Black appointments and dismissals at the University. ...Look for the next issue.*

Following the widespread circulation of the *"Black Dispatch,"* many of the faculty wrote and circulated their versions of the truth regarding departmental governance. The BAS began its inquisition. A community-based group, chaired by an attorney, conducted an investigation. Players in this governance game classified each other as "house and field niggers." Angry participants signaled their commitments by references to "death, if needs be to resolve this shit."

The Department's destructive fires burned so hotly that, by the end of July 1973, Fela Sowande had resigned. An effort was made to appoint a faculty member from a nearby institution, but that failed following significant Black on Black confrontations. As a compromise, a Black Social Work professor, Anne Jones, was eventually appointed Acting Chair. The die was cast however and, over the coming years, the Department would shrink significantly in size, scope, and productivity.

Watching the Department implode was one of my most painful experiences at Pitt. Just how painful it was became clear to me one summer day in 1973 when, while parking outside the Black Studies office, I began to cry uncontrollably. Quite concerned about my mental health, I drove around for about a half hour while tears flowed freely.

I cried profusely when I recalled how it took one of our faculty members only a few days to spend his monthly salary on dope. We revolutionaries could not tolerate an addict on the faculty. Since I could not deal with the "White pig police officers," I sought assistance from several community-based Black revolutionaries. Our private meeting lasted only a few minutes. After explaining the circumstances, I was asked, "Are you a revolutionary?" After I answered "yes," I was told, "Then do what a revolutionary has to do." With that dodging of responsibility, the meeting was over.

When I confronted the drug using faculty member, their response was, "Young blood, I don't want to have to kill you. If you fired me, I would have to kill you. Because I love you and don't want to kill you, I will resign." After the resignation letter was signed, we both cried. Before departing, the faculty member said, "You might not believe me, but you will find out that some of your revolutionary friends have been getting high with me."

Already disappointed with so much about the Department, I didn't want to believe him. In less than a year, however, I learned that he had spoken the truth. Our internal contradictions spoke so loudly that the following thoughts occurred to me: "If the White racists leave us alone, then we will self-destruct" and it was nightmarish to believe that Whites might figure this out.

Black (or as it is now often named, Africana) Studies today will remain a fragmented entity unless those responsible for implementation accept the fact that a single Department cannot conduct teaching and research related to the full scope of the African Diaspora any more than a single Department could conduct teaching and research related to the European Diaspora. Instead, a nationally recognized research University demands that there be high quality Africana/Black Studies Department narrowly tailored to focus on something such as Black American History or Black American Literature and staffed by faculty capable of achieving national recognition.

In addition to Departments, the pursuit of the African Diasporic experience will be aided by Centers such as [1] Pitt's Center for African American Poetry and Poetics which "...is a creative think tank for African American and African diasporic poetries and poetics. Our mission is to highlight, promote, and share the poetry and poetic work of African American writers..." and [2] Pitt's Center for Urban Education where "...students, faculty and colleagues learn more about student experiences, teacher roles and classroom techniques, school structure and administrative policy, announcing our progress with research and community involvement is key..."

Finally, there is the need for faculty throughout the University to diversify their courses by adding content related to the various races, religions, and other cultural demographics at the University. On that score, Pitt has appropriately provided Diversity in the Curriculum Awards which "...celebrate and reward Pitt faculty who have participated in the Provost's Diversity Institute for Faculty Development or in the University Center for Teaching and Learning's faculty development programs in diversity, and who are making diversity and inclusiveness a part of their teaching practice." Sponsored by the Office of the Provost and the University Center for Teaching and Learning, the awards recognize excellence in areas such as updated curriculum, expanded cultural awareness, development of teaching methods that are especially inclusive and interactive, consciously created learning environments that are welcoming and inclusive, and other changes that positively impact aspects of diversity and inclusion in the classroom."

CHAPTER THIRTEEN:

The Bumpy Path to Senior Administration

We Black revolutionary students, faculty, and staff members were so caught up in the "flash of gold" we recently "panned" that we did not see the built-in difficulties associated with a student-led social movement. They started to become clear when each annual election of BAS officers produced students with different priorities related to their mission, goals, and tactics as well as the specific points enumerated in the demands made to Chancellor Posvar.

Whereas their predecessors were plain and simple "Black," the newly elected BAS leaders spent inordinate amounts of time debating things such as whether their collective identity term should be "Blacks," "Afro-Americans," "African Americans," or "Nubians." Some remained proud of being "Negroes." Still others clung to "Colored" as in the National Association for the Advancement of Colored People.

The collective identity debates were complemented by arguments related to whether the best ideology was that articulated by Black Nationalists, Cultural Nationalists, Marxists, Afrocentrists, Integrationists, or some combination of these and/or other views —all of which distracted from initiatives related to obtaining more Black students, faculty, staff and administrators at Pitt.

Another shortcoming of relying on student activists emanated from the fact that the institutionally empowered BAS leaders had neither the expertise nor the time to perform tasks for which full-time faculty, staff, and administrators were needed. For example, the BAS members demanded that they be involved with the recruitment of Black students. In what now seems to be a rather duplicitous fashion, administrators sanctioned the students' absences from classes so that they could attend off-campus recruiting fairs. Time spent recruiting, along with time spent with other campus activities, meant time away from the performance of their BAS duties and, more importantly, failure to adequately address their academic work and, in turn, their grades declined precipitously.

It became clear to me that significant change at the University would come only when Blacks were no longer simply the leaders of race-related programs with meager resources and when they were on the outside of University decision making. We Blacks in the academic sector were dealing with a few hundred thousands of dollars while our counterparts throughout the University were often dealing with a multi-million-dollar enterprises. At the same time, Blacks had little if anything to do with the multi-million-dollar business side of the University.

For systemic institutional change, Blacks needed people on the Board of Trustees and they needed to serve in roles such as Chancellor, Provost, Dean, Vice President, Director, or Chair of significant units. They needed to make decisions about all aspects of Admissions and Financial Aid, not just have inputs regarding the recruitment and admission of a few hundred Black students. Hence, I thought it best that I quickly acquire skills and experiences for assuming a senior leadership position at major White colleges and universities. An opportunity for me to pursue this approach developed after a brief conversation with a middle-aged White male, Dave Powers, who had been recently promoted to Associate Provost and had been supportive when I sought his advice.

I jokingly said, "Hey Dave, how is it that White guys get promoted so easily at Pitt and no Blacks can move up the ladder?" He blushed, offered a long explanation regarding his experience and the needs of the Provost's Office, and ended with, "You know how the saying goes. I was also probably just the right guy in the right place at the right time."

Getting to my real interest, I asked, "Well, what does a guy like me have to do to get a similar chance?" Quickly, he offered, "I know just the thing for you. You would be a great intern for the American Council on Education (ACE). It sponsors an administrative Fellows Program every year. Home institutions provide a year-long administrative leave while the Fellow has an internship with a senior administrator at a host institution. Let me check with the Provost and see if we can get you nominated."

A few days later, Provost Rhoten Smith invited me to make an ACE application. Based on supporting letters from him as well as the Chancellor, my resume, and my three-page letter of intent, ACE subsequently invited me to participate in a two-day final selection screening in Washington D. C., along with about 100 other nominees. Weeks later, I was informed that I was one of those selected and that Stanford University would serve as my host institution.

The 1973–74 academic year at Stanford gave me tremendous insights regarding American higher education in general and the administration of a high-quality institution in particular. For example, my understanding of institutional mission was enhanced when a Stanford Vice Provost requested that I prepare a position paper on the then increasingly popular concept of a "university without walls." Experimental institutions such as Antioch College and the University of Massachusetts, Amherst were appealing to new students with their emphasis on experiential education, self-designed programs for students of various ages and backgrounds, independent study, interdisciplinary learning, and a de-emphasis on traditional means of assessment such as grades and examinations.

A lively discussion took place when my paper was discussed by the 99% White Deans Council and, given the many positive comments, I looked forward to meeting with the Vice Provost to talk about next steps. Our short meeting consisted of him telling me that there would be no subsequent actions related to my paper. Observing the puzzled look on my face, he said, "Let me explain something to you. Stanford is a great institution because Stanford has walls. You need to understand better the importance of the concept of institutional mission. If we forget our mission, we will cease to be Stanford."

I countered with, "But what about the poor Black students in nearby East Palo Alto? Other than not wanting to change, or possibly racism, why must a Stanford education be limited to high achieving students from primarily rich, White, conservative families instead of making it possible for some of the East Palo Alto Black kids to enroll?"

Without hesitating, he answered, "You know, there are a number of historically Black institutions that have missions related to serving Black students and, if that is what you want, perhaps that is where you should go. However, if you want to learn more about a first-class research institution with an international reputation, then there is a lot more that you can learn here. But it is all up to you."

I appreciated his frankness with me, and considered him to be very supportive of my aspirations. Knowing that it was indeed my choice, I shifted to the difficulties of my fitting in at Stanford by asking, "In terms of my getting what I can from Stanford, does it bother you or others that I don't wear suits on campus?"

He chuckled and said, "Jack, I'm a tenured faculty member and a senior academic administrator at a major research university. On a given day, I might talk with a faculty member who has a pending patent potentially worth millions, an alumnus who might wish to donate millions, or a Stanford graduate who just returned from completing her Rhodes scholarship. Therefore, I wear my suit and tie until I am relaxed at home. You are much younger, with your career ahead of you. It's like I told you about the historically Black colleges. You have to decide what you want to do."

Over the next few days, I thought considerably about the kinds of changes I was willing to make in order to succeed within a White academic administration. Would I "dress for success?" Would I learn their rituals associated with "schmoozing?" Would I accommodate my views by agreeing to the pursuit of Black Studies as courses within a traditional department as opposed to an independent department? Would it be better if I simply moved to a historically Black institution? A discussion with a Stanford Dean tipped the balance for me.

I appreciated the no nonsense approach the Dean demonstrated at Deans Council meetings. He seemed quite comfortable with his status, and he was less guarded in his comments to senior administrators. Hence, I scheduled a lunch meeting with him to discuss the relative merits of the violent student protests occurring across the country. He listened carefully, without eating, as I cited instances whereby the administration did essentially nothing until the students engaged in extreme tactics. Eventually, I quoted Frederick Douglass' statements, "If there is no struggle there is no progress. Those who profess to favor freedom, and deprecate agitation, are men who want crops without plowing up the ground, they want rain without thunder and lightning."

Finally, the Dean spoke. "Yes, but you see, America is like a pillow. If all that you do is punch it, it will bounce right back. The students are simply punching and the administrations will bounce right back after they make token responses." Recalling my frustration with making changes at Pitt, I conceded the point.

Then he added, "It is very hard for people to listen to you if you are pinching them the whole time that you are talking. Try a softer approach when you are advocating for social causes. Jack, it's up to you. You can call me a racist, a racist son of a bitch, a red neck, or whatever and, under certain circumstances, you might force me to do a few small things. But what makes you think, in the long run, I'm going to be supportive of any major project you wish to pursue?"

The Dean concluded with, "You'll probably get further by working within the system than standing outside and throwing stones. You would be better off being the Dean than protesting to the Dean. As Provost, Deans would have to listen to you since you would control their resources. Learn as much as you can while you are here, and watch where it will get you."

Persuaded by his advice, I proceeded to study in-depth Stanford's faculty tenure and promotion review processes. I had heard Pitt administrators speak of "quality" and was aware of their being teased about aspiring to become "Harvard on the Allegheny River." At Stanford, I closely observed the type of faculty quality Pitt aspired to have, and that helped me to put Pitt in a better institutional perspective. That is, notwithstanding its centuries of existence, I understood more specifically why Pitt was no Harvard or Stanford.

For example, Stanford did not look to Pitt when they recruited faculty. I was especially taken by the fact that, at the time of a tenure decision, Stanford faculty members not only needed to meet the institutional standards for research, teaching, and service, but were also required to be among if not the best qualified persons available among their colleagues from other institutions. Pitt only required that one meet its stated guidelines, but Stanford people were routinely compared with the top ten or fewer scholars in their respective fields. Given that it had existed for centuries and was still not a leading research university, I realized that Pitt's leaders were not in much of a position to berate their youthful Black Studies scholars for not having achieved more national recognition. For years to come, Stanford remained my benchmark for the realization of academic excellence.

Before returning to Pitt in September 1974, Provost Rhoten A. Smith offered and I accepted the position of Associate Dean of the College of Arts and Sciences (CAS). At that time, the CAS Dean was responsible for administering the academic rules and regulations pertaining to approximately 8,000 undergraduates. During our discussions regarding my future at Pitt, I made it known to Provost Smith that I did not want to participate in the highly contested Black Studies governance issues and, therefore, asked that my faculty position be transferred to the Department of Speech and Theatre Arts. Following the appropriate University review procedures, my faculty appointment was changed, effective September, 1974. My courses, "Black Rhetoric" and "Blacks and the Mass Media," were cross-listed with both Departments.

For the next three years, as Associate Dean, I provided advice to the CAS Dean on a variety of administrative matters pertaining to CAS' academic rules and regulations, and curricular changes. Simultaneously, from that administrative vantage point, I became the de facto "diversity officer," particularly on all matters related to Black Arts and Sciences students.

I believed things were going very well for me as a mainstream, second-tier administrator, but I found out exactly where I stood when the CAS Dean decided to leave his post at the end of June, 1978. The senior administration opted to conduct an internal search. I promptly applied for the position, noting to various decision makers that I had served four years as the Associate Dean, almost four years as a Department chair, had gained valuable experience during my years as an ACE Fellow at Stanford, and was the person most often called upon regarding diversity issues. In addition, I was of the opinion that I was in a favored position given the many times the University administrators had expressed their willingness to appoint a highly qualified Black, "if only we can find one." Well, here I was as easy to "find" as when they "found" me to head Black Studies.

As the search process unfolded, I was even more encouraged when I learned that my most serious competitor had no comparable administrative experience. In mid-June, I received a telephone call from the office of the senior administrator making the decision, and was informed that someone else had been selected, although I had "stellar qualifications." The other person was deemed a "better fit." My voice quivered, I hung up the telephone, and began to curse loudly. My secretary ran into my office, and asked, "Did something happen to one of your children?"

Hurt, angry and embarrassed, I yelled, "No!" and began gathering my personal effects. Of all that next transpired, I only remember the following exchange.

"Dr. Daniel, where are you going?"

"I don't know. You just tell those sons of bitches that I left, don't know when I'll be back, and they better not fuck with my money while I am gone!"

As the secretary stood stunned and silent, I called my wife and said, "I just quit. I'm walking out of my office now and will be home shortly."

I never returned to the CAS Dean's office as a staff member. Without telling anyone at Pitt other than Vice Provost Henderson, my family and I departed for my in-laws' home in Sacramento California. As painful as the things were that led to me crying over Black Studies, the hurt I now felt was much worse. Other than racial or some personal set of circumstances unknown to me, I could not fathom why they had hired a White male who had no comparable administrative experiences. However, the far deeper hurt came from realizing the extent to which I had trusted the Pitt administrators to "do the right thing" when it came to me. Privately, I vowed to never again place my faith so freely in Pitt.

The possibility of litigation crossed my mind, but I was so embarrassed by the rejection that I didn't want the attendant public discussion. I didn't want the shame that would come from the revolutionary brothers and sisters who most assuredly would comment "See what happens when dumb niggers trust White folks." A formally funny joke now seemed not to be so funny.

A heavy drinking, womanizing Black male was walking home one evening after a night of carousing. He got lost and stumbled over a cliff. As he was falling, he grabbed a tree branch, held on, and began praying to God. God heard him and asked, "My dear son, do you really believe in God?"

Desperate and now sober, the guy said, "Yes Lord, yes Lord, I've seen the evil of my ways. Save me, Lord, and I will serve you the rest of my days." God then said, "Okay, if you really believe, then quit holding that branch and I will save you." The guy let go, started falling, and seconds before he hit the stones below, he heard God say, "Dumb Nigger."

I now felt like that dumb nigger for having believed that I need only work hard, get the right experiences, modify my decorum, and the University administrators would be supportive of me. I had done my prescribed job and done even more as the de facto diversity officer. I thought my parents were right when they and other senior Blacks claimed that by working harder, faster, and better than White people we could get ahead. In my opinion, Malcolm X was right. A Black with a PhD in nuclear physics and living in Mississippi was still a nigger and the same was true in the minds of some regarding me at Pitt!

Throughout July and most of August, I refused to answer telephone calls from Pitt administrators inquiring about my intentions. Then, to my great surprise, the person to whom the Dean of CAS reported, Dean Jerome L. Rosenberg, sent a letter offering me a position as his Associate. Still angry and hurt, I refused to answer the letter. Finally, toward the end of August, Vice Provost Henderson called and said, "Look man. They're about to fire your ass. They've made you a heck of an offer and you need to get back to them. They asked me to call you man, and that's what I've done. I understand how you feel, but think about your future and let's talk some more when you return."

With my wife needing to return to her job in September, two young children, and having no other employment alternatives, I accepted my new position as Associate Dean of the Faculty of Arts and Sciences (FAS), effective September 1, 1978. I did so with considerable distrust and very mixed emotions.

My new supervisor, Dean Rosenberg, was viewed by many in Black Studies as their arch enemy. He was the one with whom the disagreements took place regarding the Department's budgets, as well as the person who presided over the processes that led to the denial of tenure and promotion to a number of faculty members recommended by the Department. During the many confrontations with him, there were efforts to break into his office and steal confidential letters related to controversial Black Studies tenure decisions. On another occasion, Black faculty and students took him hostage, and demanded without success that he reverse some of his decisions regarding Black Studies. Now, most importantly for me, he had participated in making the decision to not appoint me as the CAS Dean.

In my new position, I served as Dean Rosenberg's primary staff person for reviewing and making recommendations regarding budgets totaling $4.5 million for summer faculty instruction; and conducting initial reviews of faculty tenure and promotion dossiers; and reviewing faculty recruitment requests. As such, I was in constant contact with the leadership of the largest and most central academic unit of the University. Without realizing what had transpired, I had again been thrown into the "briar patch." Arts and Sciences included the largest number of Black faculty and staff, the largest Black student access program, and the Black Studies Department. As was the case when I worked in CAS, I was once again the de facto diversity officer, but operated from a much more powerful administrative base.

Over time, Dean Rosenberg became one of the Pitt administrators I most admired. He was the one who best pursued the standards of faculty achievement I observed at Stanford. He best illustrated how to use the budget to strategically support his unit's mission and highest academic priorities. He was the Dean who was most successful in resisting budget cuts imposed by the Provost and Chancellor. He was also the one who never wavered when activists attempted to cajole him with fear tactics. Also, of great importance to me was his support for race-related issues when they were linked to the Arts and Sciences mission and performed in a high-quality fashion.

Rosenberg's support of my University-wide efforts from 1978 through the mid–1980s permitted me to be involved with the recruitment of most Black faculty and administrative positions in and outside of the Arts and Sciences. There was no major Black student issue for which the senior University administration and/ or the BAS did not seek my advice. Similarly, concerned members of the local Black community often consulted with me, including K. Leroy Irvis, Pennsylvania's first Black Speaker of the House of Representatives. It was also at this time that I became Chair of Equipoise, the University's formally recognized organization of Black staff, faculty and administrators.

Still, more than a year later, I was unable to reach emotional closure regarding not having been appointed the CAS Dean. It took the reading of a passage by James Baldwin, in his "Letter to My Nephew on the One Hundredth Anniversary of Emancipation" to finally stop my being tormented by that sting.

In his letter, Baldwin told his nephew that he was born into a situation where he was not expected to aspire to excellence but to accept mediocrity, to accept the negative things Whites said about his inferiority. Further, Baldwin stated that such Whites were trapped in their beliefs regarding the inferiority of Blacks, too frightened of the consequences of changing their views. He added:

> *Try to imagine how you would feel if you woke up one morning to find the sun shining and all the stars aflame. You would be frightened because it is out of the order of nature. Any upheaval in the universe is terrifying because it so profoundly attacks one's sense of one's own reality. Well, the black man has functioned in the white man's world as a fixed star, as an immovable pillar: and as he moves out of his place, heaven and earth are shaken to their foundations."*

The foregoing passage provided me with some, but not complete, psychological relief to realize that Jack L. Daniel was a fixed star in the minds of many White powers that be at Pitt. Jack L. Daniel was an angry, militant, young, unpredictable, and, to make matters worse, educated Black male —the very bête noire feared by so many Whites. My mistake was to have believed that Whites would accept me for whom I had become.

At the time, I didn't believe I was the "prophet" who could not be heard in his "own land." It seemed to be a very misguided hope that Pitt could become "my land," that its people could become "my people." Just as I received limited acceptance by playing Bridge as a student while at UPJ, the same was true of my administrative career at Pitt – "one of us" did not apply to me no matter how well I played the administrative game. Hence, I set out on a different course of action. Instead of acceptance, I would make myself so valuable to the institution as a whole that it would have to be supportive of my goals related to Blacks.

CHAPTER FOURTEEN:

The John Henry Years

John Henry said to his captain,
A man is nothing but a man,
But before I let your steam drill beat me down,
I'd die with a hammer in my hand, Lord, Lord,
I'd die with a hammer in my hand.

Although I experienced a significant degree of professional satisfaction while serving as an academic administrator, like a recurring nightmare, the CAS Dean rejection and its attendant emotional impact continued to haunt me. To end obsessing about the matter, again I planned to retreat to the comfort of being a full-time faculty member. However, in 1983, my plans took a completely unexpected turn after the University hired Provost Roger Benjamin.

Benjamin immediately began a University-wide strategic planning initiative which soon had the University's top administrators buzzing about strategic planning factors such as "quality," "centrality," "comparative advantage," and "cost-effectiveness." Bothered by the fact that Provost Benjamin had made no major public pronouncements regarding race-related matters and, fearing that he might make major decisions without attending to these issues, I wrote him a several page letter.

Enjoying the use of his planning concepts to make my case, I argued that we had a comparative advantage given the size of our regional and national Black student applicant pool and, as such, we could certainly enroll and retain Black students in a cost-effective fashion. After presenting details regarding what I perceived to be the state of the Black administrative, faculty, staff, and curricular presence at the University, I ended with a request to meet with Benjamin at his earliest convenience.

Benjamin called several days later, invited me to meet with him, and immediately tipped his hand with, "Jack, I could really use you in my office. You have precisely the academic values and work experience I'm looking for to help move this University to first class status. Together, we could accomplish a lot."

Caught completely off guard, I responded, "What specifically is it that you believe we could accomplish? And, before you answer, you should know that I'm planning to get out of administration as soon as I can."

Benjamin replied, "Why would you do that, Jack, given what you wrote in your letter to me? You seem to know exactly what needs to be done and I'm offering to partner with you. You just need the right platform here at the University. Look, I need strong leadership in undergraduate education and you could be that person, serving as an Assistant Provost for Undergraduate Programs. The job is yours and you can start right away."

During an hour of discussion, Benjamin outlined a major portfolio that included serving as his liaison to Pitt's four undergraduate regional campus Presidents. I would also [1] coordinate the Provost's Office review of proposed major changes to undergraduate programs; [2] serve as the Provost's Office contact person for matters pertaining to peer and student evaluation of teaching; [3] be the person to whom the Director of Academic Support for Student Athletes as well as the Director of Admissions and Financial Aid reported; and [4] help him to formulate University responses to diversity issues. A week later, in yet another rather serendipitous fashion, I extended my administrative relationship with Pitt.

I remained in the Provost's Office from 1984 through 2005 and, during those 21 years, served under 5 different Provosts. For much of my first ten years in that Office, the revolving door of the Provost position adversely impacted efforts to sustain initiatives related to Blacks at the University. For example, I had been an Assistant Provost for less than a year before rumors circulated regarding the possibility of Benjamin leaving Pitt which he in fact did before we could articulate and implement a major program related to Blacks.

Similarly, Provost Weingartner (1986-89) barely completed three years of service before he vacated the post. During his administration, we did implement a procedure whereby, on his behalf, I reviewed the search processes to determine if sufficient efforts had been made to attract a pool of diverse candidates for proposed new faculty appointments. Although the process contributed to a few more women and people of color being in the applicant pools, it was also the case that most often the search committee proposed and received approval to hire a White male with far superior credentials.

Throughout the changes in the Provost's Office leadership, my general portfolio continued to expand as I was promoted from Assistant to Associate to Vice Provost, served as the de facto diversity officer, and continued to publish scholarly articles and teach a course each term. During these years, I did not pay much attention to the fact that I performed the "Super Nigger" role of working harder, running faster, and always doing more than twice as much to maintain similar jobs held by Whites. It was Interim Provost Nordenberg who caused me to ponder the extent of my administrative engagement. He asked the Vice Provosts to provide him with updates on their respective portfolios and, after doing so, he privately called my attention to the fact that my workload far exceeded that of the other Vice Provosts.

I wasn't bothered by my workload because I believed I had become the "real diner" Malcolm X referenced in his 1961 "Ballot or the Bullet" Speech. In that speech, Malcolm declared,

> *Well, I am one who doesn't believe in deluding myself. I'm not going to sit at your table and watch you eat, with nothing on my plate, and call myself a diner. Sitting at the table doesn't make you a diner, unless you eat some of what's on that plate. Being here in America doesn't make you an American. Being born here in America doesn't make you an American. Why, if*

*birth made you American, you wouldn't need any legislation;
you wouldn't need any amendments to the Constitution; you
wouldn't be faced with civil-rights filibustering in Washington,
D.C., right now. They don't have to pass civil-rights legislation
to make a Polack an American.*

I was fully involved, a true diner, under Henderson (1989–93)
and Nordenberg (1993–94) when it came to major matters such as
[1] my coordination of the review and approval process related to
the University's creation of a new undergraduate Business program
and an Honors College; [2] serving as the Provost's deputy for major
units such as the School of Education, Law, Arts and Sciences, and
Engineering; [3] coordinating the critically important enrollment
management for the Provost's Office; and, at the same time, [4]
spearheading the Provosts' diversity programs for Blacks and women.

Under Provost Maher (1994-2005), I continued to view myself as
a real "diner" with more than plenty on my plate. For example, this
was the case when I literally did two full-time jobs by simultaneously
serving as Vice Provost and Interim Dean of the College of General
Studies (CGS) at which time I engaged in significant restructuring
of CGS. Subsequently, notwithstanding other administrative search
committees' failure to find Black and women candidates, I chaired
the search committees that led to the appointment of the first
Black male and, subsequently, a White female permanent College
of General Studies Dean.

I had the same sense of professional well-being when I next
simultaneously held two full-time jobs while serving as Vice Provost
and Dean of Student Affairs. With the full support of the central
administration, I made major organizational changes in Student
Affairs. At the same time, I significantly improved the Black staff
presence in Student Affairs by appointing a Black woman as Assistant
Dean; a Black woman as Assistant to the Dean; and a Black male
as the Director of a major unit. For these and other reasons, I was
extremely proud of myself as a "mainstream diner" and believed
that I could, like the mythical John Henry, beat the "steam engine,"
that is, succeed in making massive changes related to Blacks while

functioning in a historically White institution that was very slow to make such changes.

As a "steel driving man" throughout the 1990s at Pitt, I received tremendous satisfaction from providing Black students with the critical support they needed to succeed at Pitt. This included administering the following Provost Office's funds: [1] the Provost's Development Fund facilitated minority and women students' completion of doctoral degrees by providing them with dissertation support; [2] the Commonwealth Fund was used to enhance the recruitment, retention and graduation of disadvantaged students, particularly Blacks; [3] the Graduate Tuition and Stipend Fund provided graduate support for students who helped the University realize its graduate student diversity mission; and [4] the Special Projects fund was used to fund an array of one-time new initiatives such as Post-doctoral fellowships, emergency living expenses, books for financially needy students, travel to recruit students, recruiting materials, and other forms of student aid.

During my "John Henry" years, I was formally offered the opportunity to become Provost at one institution and Associate Chancellor at another, but opted to remain at Pitt largely because of the support the senior administration provided for initiatives related to Black students. For example, from a modest beginning of less than $200,000 annually in 1984, by 2004 these funds grew to nearly $3 million per year during Maher's administration. Annually, hundreds of Black students received assistance which contributed directly to their retention and graduation.

Working directly with the Director of Admission and Financial Aid (OAFA) provided a significant opportunity for me to further my Black student agenda. The Board of Trustees' facilitated this effort when it passed a February 22, 1996 resolution which indicated in part,

> ...To achieve a more desirable programmatic balance, to fulfill its institutional mission and to increase its overall stature, it is essential that the University place special emphasis on undergraduate education in the months and years ahead. More specifically, it is necessary that attention, energy, and

appropriate resources be devoted to ...increasing recent suc-
cesses in attracting, retaining and graduating a more diverse
(multicultural, racial, geographic, etc.) undergraduate student
body..." Moreover, the Board directs the Chancellor to proceed
...with the highest sense of urgency and recommend to the
Board of Trustees, by December 31, 1996, a plan and time-
table for addressing each of the above areas...

Signaling our intent to improve undergraduate education and, simultaneously strengthening relationships with the local Black community, I articulated and Provost Maher as well as Chancellor Nordenberg approved full room, board and tuition scholarships which carried the names of the very prominent local Blacks, i.e., Helen Faison, Robert Lavelle, Adena Davis, and Donald M. Henderson. At any given point beginning in the mid-1990s, there were approximately 55 of these Black student scholars in residence. The vast majority of them achieved at very high academic levels, went on to the very best graduate and professional schools, pursued distinguished careers, and aided the University in improving the overall standing of its first-year student retention.

Nevertheless, with each passing year, I became increasingly sensitive to the fact that, by playing my John Henry role, I inadvertently contributed to a situation whereby other institutional leaders focused less on the agenda related to Blacks because, "We have Jack doing that, and he does it so well." To make matters worse, there was no known possibility of someone on campus replacing me should I withdraw my fingers from the many holes in the diversity "dike." The vast majority of the Vice Provost's positions were filled by internal candidates and, because no other Black American at Pitt had my type of professional history, there was no one prepared and willing to succeed me. In one instance, I facilitated the hiring of a Black female Vice Provost, but she soon left the Office.

With no prospect for internal succession planning, I decided to take steps to shore up what I deemed to be my highest priority, i.e., the recruitment, retention, and graduation of Black students. To accomplish this, I first obtained Chancellor Nordenberg's and

Provost Maher's approval to conduct an assessment of the current campus circumstances related to Black students. My work led to the 1997 report, "A 21st Century African American Student Agenda: A Matter of Higher Expectations," which I submitted to Chancellor Nordenberg and Provost Maher and, subsequently, had critiqued by a group of Black faculty and staff members.

Much of what I recommended was based on our recent success in enrolling and graduating academically high achieving Black students as compared to our institutional history of enrolling primarily "disadvantaged students" through programs supported by the federal government, the Commonwealth of Pennsylvania, and the University. The largest disadvantaged student program, located in the Arts and Sciences, was known as the University Challenge to Excellence Program (UCEP). The smaller Impact Program was located in Engineering.

No matter what euphemism was used, the fact remained that most 1960s through the mid-1990s Black students entered the University with significantly lower academic qualifications based on standardized indices and, most importantly to me, they graduated at abysmal rates. For example, the available data for students who entered between 1985 and 1992 indicated the following:

- After four years   Blacks 17.1%   Whites 39.4%;
- After five years   Blacks 35.8%   Whites 61.8%; and
- After six years   Blacks 41.3%   Whites 66.4%.

I was also deeply troubled by the very low "C" cumulative grade point averages of so many of the Black graduates given that the overall grade point average of graduating seniors was greater than a "B." Additionally, all too many of the Blacks who failed to graduate left the University with debts amounting to tens of thousands of dollars. To continue with this strategy was tantamount to what George W. Bush termed the "soft bigotry of low expectations" or, possibly worse, economic exploitation.

A few Black staff rationalized the very low Black student academic outcomes by arguing that, given much lower entry qualifications, the above Black student outcomes were reasonable. I responded that it was morally wrong, given decades of experience, to continue a strategy that resulted in so few students graduating and many leaving heavily indebted. Moreover, it was not the provision of opportunity that I opposed, but rather I stressed the importance of Black student access to *and* success at Pitt.

We needed a modern, 21*st* Century strategy that would lead to many more Black graduates with much higher cumulative grade point averages in a much wider array of academic disciplines. Therefore, I concluded my 1997 report as follows: "…To move forward, there must be zero tolerance at all levels for mediocrity… When it comes to 'bench-marking,' our goal must be for us to occupy a leadership position among the very best AAU institutions."

Chancellor Nordenberg and Provost Maher embraced the fundamental recommendations of my report which included [1] recruiting a cohort of academically talented Black students; [2] having all academic units institute programs to address the "pipeline" issues --dropping out, stopping out, and low performance by Black students from pre-school through undergraduate school; [3] developing creative uses of financial aid to support diversity; [4] making the recruitment, retention and graduation of Black students a shared responsibility, not just the responsibility of Blacks in special programs and Black faculty members; [5] realizing better use of existing resources committed to diversity; and [6] determining students to be the highest priority for diversity programs. After my presentation to the Deans Council, its members also embraced the goal of taking steps to get Blacks achieving, minimally, at the same levels of White students.

Over the next four years, a team of Provost's Office administrators worked with the Admissions and Financial Aid staff to recruit high achieving Black students and, simultaneously, increase the number of Black students on campus. External validation came by way of the 2002 Middle States report which included the following statements,

> …*The University shows a strong commitment to the recruitment, retention, and graduation of historically underrepresented students, and has achieved success in increasing student diversity, particularly with African-Americans.* …

The University takes pride in the fact that retention rates are higher now than at any time in the 1990s. The retention rates for first-time freshmen entering in Fall Term 1999 are 85.2%. The comparable retention rate for minority students is 84%, the highest since 1985, the earliest year for which data exist.

Still, I worried about things falling apart once I left the Provost's Office. I didn't know if senior administrators simply put their heads in the sand regarding a possible planned succession, if they believed and/or hoped that I would never quit my administrative posts during their tenure, or if there were other motivations for not proactively addressing my eventual departure. What I did know was that I was aging, tiring, and worrying more each year about a wide range of very disappointing facts related to the Black presence at Pitt, even though significant successes were being realized with students.

In 2004, it was very disturbing to note that from its beginnings in 1787 through the first part of the twenty-first century only White men had served as Chancellor; Provost with one exception; Deans of most units; most of the Department Chairs; and the vast majority of the tenured faculty. During the 2004-05 academic year, for example, there were more than 110 academic Department Chairs and or Division Heads. Of the total, there were only 19 women. A Black male served as Chair of the Africana Studies Department. A Black woman served as Chair of the Department of Family Medicine.

After nearly four decades of struggle, a particularly appalling set of data related to Black faculty indicated the following:

- In 1971, there were 57 tenured and tenure-stream Black faculty.
- In 1974, there were 72 tenured and tenure-stream Black faculty.
- In 2004, there were 54 tenured and tenure-stream Black faculty.

Still worse, a significant number of the Black faculty members were nearing retirement, a fact that, were it true of the entire faculty, would cause panic for the senior administration. To my dismay, there was no foreseeable change in the Black faculty situation.

Preoccupied with these and other concerns related to Blacks at Pitt, a gloomy set of thoughts came to me while I was listening to a futuristic discussion during a Deans Council meeting. As Deans described where they thought their respective units would be in five years, I began to ponder the probability that, in five years, I would no longer be sitting at the Deans Council table. My mind wandered from the Deans' discussion, and a nightmarish daydream unfolded.

There was a chorus of mocking voices laughing at me as I engaged in what seemed to be a futile effort. At first it seemed as though I was Sisyphus sentenced to push a huge diversity stone up a hill that seemed higher than Pitt's forty-story Cathedral of Learning. Gradually the Sisyphus image darkened and I imagined that I was more like John Henry after he had beaten the steam driving machine. After decades of hammering, would I too simply lay down my hammer and die and, still worse, without having beaten the "steam engine" –having Pitt become a national model for diversity and inclusion related to Blacks?

Throughout the next several days, mulling over my long-term relationship with Pitt became a major preoccupation if not an obsession. I was especially bothered by the fact that, while partnering with the administration, our institutional reputation grew nationally and internationally. I had played significant roles in helping Pitt become widely known as a place that got it right when it came to right sizing; building a distinguished faculty; increasing the quality of the student body; significantly improving undergraduate education; enhancing Student Affairs; improving the quality of teaching; and providing high quality comprehensive support services for student athletes. Yet, when it came to hiring Black faculty, senior administrators and staff, there was not the same degree of institutional or personal success and it seemed, institutionally speaking, that Black folks were expected to accept a few sporadic successes that came at a "horse and buggy" pace.

I stumbled through my administrative work for three more years before the mental weight brought me to a halt. As B. B. King put it in his blues song, "the thrill was gone." It was painfully clear that by playing the "John Henry" role I might realize some additional successes with Black students but, when it came to significantly adding to the Black faculty, administrator and staff presence, I was less hopeful. Knowing I had run my administrative course with Pitt, I submitted my resignation as Vice Provost, effective December 31, 2005.

Instead of the flawed "John Henry" approach, since my retirement and led by the new Chancellor Patrick Gallagher as of 2018, Pitt has made progress by hiring [1] a Black woman as a Senior Vice Chancellor and Secretary to the Board of Trustees; [2] a Black woman as Senior Vice Chancellor and Chief Legal Officer; [3] a Black man as the School of Engineering Dean; [4] a Black woman as the School of Education Dean; and [5] a Black man as the men's Basketball Coach. Prior to Gallagher's arrival, a White woman had been selected to serve as Provost.

Most importantly, Pitt's diversity and inclusion initiatives have become shared responsibility, not the primary province of Blacks. A stellar example was provided by the Office of Admissions and Financial Aid which reported in 2015, "This fall's freshman class is not only larger than expected, it's more diverse than ever, with the class of 2019 hailing from 44 states and 1,312 high schools, plus 17 other countries. The proportion of nonwhite freshmen — 26.2 percent — is a record for Pitt, with 1,061 minority students among the class..."

Especially important for the class of 2019, is the fact that Pitt now has a comprehensive First Year Experience initiative whose goal "...is to ensure that all new Pitt students find a welcoming and engaging community when they arrive on campus..." I had the opportunity to learn more about Pitt's comprehensive proactive retention initiatives in 2018 when I went with my son, Omari; my wife, Jerlean; and my grandson, Javon, on a campus visit. We, along with the other visiting students and their family members were deeply impressed with the comprehensive and personalized approach to integrating new students into the University and, in other ways, enabling them to succeed at the University.

CHAPTER FIFTEEN:

What Mattered Most

During my more than 3 decades of playing "John Henry" at Pitt, I worked not simply "9 to 5" but seemingly "24/7!" Significant parts of my weekends were often devoted to catching up with my administrative work in order that I be better prepared for the coming week. Having retired, I no longer had my familiar daily routines and the people with whom I most often interacted. Most importantly, my former sense of purpose was missing and, in turn, caused me to question my self-worth. My emotional foundations shook when I wondered if, during my life's work, I had done all I should have done in terms of helping Blacks succeed at Pitt. Even if I had, what was now my purpose in life? At age 63, I was immersed in retirement blues and bewildered by not knowing what I might/ should do during the "last quarter of my life."

My frustration grew especially intense one December evening. I was caught in the evening's rush hour traffic and, slowed by darkness and patches of black ice, the traffic crawled along like a giant python barely moving after having swallowed an enormous dinner. My restless finger continuously pressed the radio's seek button, rapidly skipping over stations playing rhythm and blues, light jazz, and classic Christmas songs. I stopped when I heard Nancy Wilson's satin voice singing softly but firmly, "I've Never Been to me." I listened ever so empathetically as she sang about having sipped champagne on a yacht, vacationed in celebrated places, made love in the sun, and done other presumed glamorous things but had never done what mattered most to her, i.e., "been to me." I wondered if I had "ever been to me" during my years at Pitt.

Seeking to make sense of my relationship with Pitt and, as a bit of catharsis, I began to write about my Pitt experiences, starting with when I enrolled at the University of Pittsburgh at Johnstown. Too emotionally close to the memories and related feelings that bubbled to the surface, I stopped drafting when I got to the years I spent helping to build the Black Studies Department. It took an early spring 2006 reconnection with one of my former students, Imelda, for me to begin the process of fully understanding the nature of what mattered most to me about my life's work at Pitt.

After about five minutes of indulging my sentiments related to my possible shortcomings at Pitt, Imelda looked sternly into my eyes and softly, almost sadly, stated, "You really don't know who you are, to us. You don't know the Jack we know." Caught off guard by her remarks as well as what seemed to be a bit of sadness on her face, I asked, "What do you mean? I don't know me?"

Imelda smiled knowingly and offered, "You don't see the Jack your former students see. If you ask them about yourself, your students will tell you the same thing. Actually, the fact that you don't see who we see is so interesting that you might want to call your book 'The Me I Didn't Know.' Wow, my favorite professor doesn't know himself!" Caught off guard, I sat silently as she added, "You could start by arranging another time to talk with me. Actually, you need to talk with a lot of your former students and learn about the Jack they know."

Feeling vulnerable and not sure I wanted to hear what Imelda might say next, I impulsively pulled out my telephone and responded with, "Okay, Gil is a student who knew me quite well. Let me call him and see what he has to say." I reached Gil, exchanged greetings, and then stated, "Gil, I'm sitting in Baltimore talking with a former student, Imelda, and she claims that I don't know the Jack who my students knew. So, I'm calling to find out who is the Jack you knew at Pitt?"

Gil answered, "Professor, I know exactly what's she's talking about and I'd love to go into it with you, but "I've got a meeting coming up in few minutes." I promised to send him an email and, after hanging up, agreed to do the same with Imelda. Working with the two of them, the following reconstruction of what mattered most to them and me took place. For their contributions to my salvation, I remain eternally grateful.

Throughout my administrative career, I taught one course per semester. I had valued teaching primarily because it provided me with relief from administrative work. It was also my fun time because I enjoyed lecturing and holding discussions with my students. As things turned out, these were also the occasions during which I now believe I did my most important work on behalf of my students, particularly when I taught my signature course, "Black Rhetoric."

Imelda took "Black Rhetoric" in 1976. After the first major examination, my secretary came into my office with a worried look on her face, closed the door, and said, "Dr. Daniel, one of your students is here to see you. I know you're busy doing that report for the Dean, but she said it was really important." In my normal fashion of stopping to meet with a student if they had mustered the initiative to come to my office, I replied, "Okay, I need a break from drafting this report. Send her in."

An eighteen-year-old academically talented student walked in, closed the door, and asked loudly, "Dr. Daniel! Why did I get this grade on my exam? I got all the answers correct on your mid-term exam, but you gave me a 99%." Through her consistently insightful comments in class as well as the thoroughness of her earlier short paper assignments, I had identified Imelda as a student with great intellectual ability. Hence, I merely smiled and said nothing. Now angrier, Imelda marched toward my desk and shouted, "Why did I not receive 100%?"

Appreciating greatly her fortitude, I explained, "Well, Imelda, it is important that you work as hard as you can. You still live at a time in which a racist society forces you to be 'twice as good' in order to succeed. I deducted one point for motivational purposes, to make sure that you work extra hard on your term paper and, in general, grow accustomed to performing at the highest level for which you are capable."

Still angry, she asked, "But are you testing motivation or knowledge of your subject matter? This is a course in Black Rhetoric, not motivation."

Seizing my chance to mentor her, I responded, "If you were to take me before the University's academic integrity review board, then I'd have to admit that your grade should be a function of your correct answers. However, as I said, you need proper motivation. You're a Black female and after you leave the University, life will severely test your motivation, not just your knowledge of what you learned while here. There are those who will try to hold you back simply because you are female and Black. It's not right but like that old spiritual says, 'ninety-nine and a half won't do' when it comes to Black women succeeding in America. You will need to know all of the correct answers, plus have one hundred and one percent in motivation to overcome barriers put in your path."

Squinting her eyes and forming a tear, Imelda said in a quivering voice, "All of that might be true, but Dr. Daniel, I correctly answered all of the test questions and I want my 100%. If you want to test my motivation, then give me a separate test on motivation!"

I laughed and said, "Imelda, I already did! I gave you 99% for motivational purposes. Here you are in my office, interrupting my administrative work, demanding your 100%, and refusing to take 'No' for answer. You couldn't be more highly motivated than at this moment, and so I will change your grade to 100%. Before you go, however, I want to talk with you about your plans after graduation. What's your aim in life?" We then spent almost an hour discussing her career aspirations, various majors, minors, and relevant courses.

Imelda's willingness to challenge my grading of her paper prompted me to tell her the "Eagle" story that I often told to my students to highlight the importance of knowing who they were and having self-confidence. As was the case when I enrolled at UPJ, many Black students came to Pitt through "special" programs and, regardless of euphemisms such as "disadvantaged students" and "social justice programs," they felt stigmatized. Many did not believe they were "eagles" who could "soar" by majoring in anything they wished and earning very high grades. Hence, I sought to bolster their self-esteem by telling them the following story and, in subsequent conversations, constantly reminding them that they were "eagles."

The Eagles

Once upon a time, an eagle flew over a chicken farm located in the rural Appalachian Mountains where a farmer and his family barely eked out a living. As the eagle flew over the chicken farm, one of the farmer's teenage sons used his slingshot to hit her in one wing, forcing her to land in the chicken yard. Unable to fly, the eagle eventually laid two eggs in the chicken yard.

After the eagle's eggs hatched, the young chickens began to tease the two baby eagles, Omari and Tom, for having such big feet, big flat beaks, and curly instead of straight feathers. The mother chickens refused to allow their baby daughters to play with them, much less think about dating them.

Tom got depressed and began to scrape his big claws on rocks in order to reduce them to a smaller size similar to the chickens. Next, Tom found some axle grease, rubbed it into his feathers and made them straight like chicken feathers. Tom went so far as to find a rag, tied it around his feathers to help keep them straight, and called it a 'do rag," a rag to make his feathers 'do right.' Tom even began to eat chicken feed off the ground. Soon Tom developed a little swaying walk, something he called his 'ghetto mack.'

Meanwhile, Omari kept telling Tom that he was having a recurring dream in which he somehow learned that he was not supposed to eat chicken feed off the ground. When Tom told the chickens about this part of Omari's dream, the chickens began to call Omari a 'radical Muslim.' But Omari believed in his dream and told Tom that they were special in that, one day, they would be able to fly, that they came from a royal family.

Finally, Thanksgiving came and since the poor farmer couldn't afford a turkey, he decided to kill the fattest bird on the grounds. And there was Tom with his belly hanging to the ground from eating all of that chicken feed. The farmer took Tom to the chopping block and, just as he raised his axe, a big shadow came over them. They looked up and there was Omari, flying out of the chicken yard, going on to his royal destiny. And you, Imelda, are an eagle. Don't ever let anyone turn you into a chicken! Don't let anyone tell you what you can't do at Pitt! You can reach whatever heights to which you decide to fly."

Imelda smiled and said softly but assuredly, "Yes, Dr. Daniel. I am an eagle." I understood much more fully the professorial roles I played with Imelda and many other students when she wrote the following to me in 2006.

> ...Time is a precious commodity that you gave freely. What you don't get is that most people don't take time to listen to someone in distress, let alone take action to relieve that distress. That is what you did instinctively, because of compassion and commitment to Blacks first, and then your commitment to students in general and education. I was thinking about my description of you and I said to myself, he is my Hero. At first, I thought that was a little dramatic. But then I looked up the definition of Hero which is "a man celebrated for his strength and bold exploits, and noted by many for his special achievements."

> Well that is you! What Black man is bold enough to go to a White professor and tell them to give a Black student who walked out in the middle of a test and give her a chance to redo the test? Pretty bold, don't you think? And for special achievements, how many Black students in a majority White university go from protester to executive at the same university? These are all things that keep your students like me in awe of you. You see that is the Jack you don't know. (Personal correspondence, June 27, 2006).

Staring out my second-floor office window, seeking to calm the waves of warm emotions welling up inside me, and pushing back tears of joy, I started humming one of my church favorites, "Peace be Still." Then much of what I had been doing via my teaching came rolling back to me, particularly what I did on the first day of class.

In terms of helping my students succeed, the first day of class might well have been the most important class I taught. Instead of holding low student expectations such as the "C" average UPJ had for me or the bare minimum "B" required during my first days as a graduate student, I used the first day of class to express my highest expectations for my students. I treated them as if they were "A" students and many of them behaved as if they were "A" students. The first day vehicles I used for doing so were the [1] poem "Equipment;" [2] George Washington Carver's work with peanuts; and [3] metaphors related to "peanuts, diamonds and pearls."

EQUIPMENT

FIGURE IT OUT FOR YOURSELF, MY LAD,
YOU'VE ALL THAT THE GREATEST OF MEN HAVE HAD,
TWO ARMS, TWO HANDS, TWO LEGS, TWO EYES,
AND A BRAIN TO USE IF YOU WOULD BE WISE,
WITH THIS EQUIPMENT THEY ALL BEGAN.
SO START FROM THE TOP AND SAY, "I CAN."

LOOK THEM OVER, THE WISE AND THE GREAT,
THEY TAKE THEIR FOOD FROM A COMMON PLATE,
AND SIMILAR KNIVES AND FORKS THEY USE,
WITH SIMILAR LACES THEY TIE THEIR SHOES,
THE WORLD CONSIDERS THEM BRAVE AND SMART,
BUT YOU'VE ALL THEY HAD WHEN THEY MADE THEIR START.

YOU CAN TRIUMPH AND COME TO SKILL
YOU CAN BE GREAT IF ONLY YOU WILL
YOU'RE WELL EQUIPPED FOR WHAT FIGHT YOU CHOOSE;
AND YOU HAVE ARMS AND LEGS AND A BRAIN TO USE,
AND THE MAN WHO HAS RISEN GREAT DEEDS TO DO
BEGAN HIS LIFE WITH NO MORE THAN YOU.

YOU ARE THE HANDICAP YOU MUST FACE,
YOU ARE THE ONE WHO MUST CHOOSE YOUR PLACE.
YOU MUST SAY WHERE YOU WANT TO GO,
HOW MUCH YOU WILL STUDY THE TRUTH TO KNOW;
GOD HAS EQUIPPED YOU FOR LIFE, BUT HE
LETS YOU DECIDE WHAT YOU WANT TO BE.

COURAGE MUST COME FROM THE SOUL WITHIN
THE MAN MUST FURNISH THE WILL TO WIN.
SO FIGURE IT OUT FOR YOURSELF, MY LAD,
YOU WERE BORN WITH ALL THAT THE GREAT HAVE HAD
WITH YOUR EQUIPMENT THEY ALL BEGAN,
GET HOLD OF YOURSELF AND SAY: "I CAN."

After listening to my students' comments about the poem, I informed them that George Washington Carver often recited this poem to students who doubted their abilities. Then I reminded them of the hundreds of useful products Carver made from peanuts, even though many farmers perceived them to be relatively worthless. After emphasizing that it was because Carver saw the possibilities in the peanuts that he was able to make peanut-based products as disparate as ice cream, sausage, cooking oil, peanut lemon punch, candy, soap, glycerin, dyes, rubber, and medication for Dandruff, I told my students,

> *Just as many people didn't look at peanuts properly, didn't see the potential in peanuts, many people look wrongly at you. My mother always said, 'If you look at a person wrong, you'll see them wrong.' If you look at a person as being stupid, then*

you will see them as stupid even though they may be a genius. This term, I am going to look at you as my peanuts. Surely, if Carver could get hundreds of products from peanuts, I should be able to get much more out of you since you are far more complex than a peanut. And, what you need to understand is that none of this will be possible if you don't see yourselves correctly, if you don't realize the peanut potential within you, if you don't truly believe that you have the equipment to become whatever you wish.

I followed the peanut metaphor by soliciting brief comments on the formation and use of diamonds, after which I made the following points:

Always remember that it takes extreme temperatures and tons of pressure to make a diamond, the same kinds of extreme temperatures and pressures that some of you experienced growing up in your home communities. To obtain a single carat of diamond, tons of debris must be removed. At first glance, the unseeing eye, the ill-informed professor, perceives many of you as dirt, that is, the type of student who should not have been admitted to Pitt. Yet if you remove the dirt, then you will get not only a beautiful jewel but also a very strong substance that can be used for industrial purposes.

A good professor has to be able to see a 'diamond in the rough,' to see the jewel his students are capable of becoming, to understand and facilitate their growth potential. I'm going to assume that I have a room full of peanuts and diamonds. Even if someone in this room is on academic probation, I'm still assuming that this diamond in the rough will be an "A+" student once they realize the potential they have as a peanut, as a diamond. You only need, as the poem urges, get a hold of yourselves and say I can.

Next, I dove into a discussion of pearls and emphasized the fact that a tiny grain of sand entered the oyster's systems, irritated the oyster's "system," and unable to get rid of the source of irritation, the oyster secreted a substance around the tiny grand of sand turning it into a pearl. Then I likened my students to tiny grains of sand, and urged them to figure out for themselves which of society's systems they wanted to enter and agitate until those systems turned them into pearls.

I ended the first day by reinforcing my perception of students as human beings in the process of becoming whatever they willed. Speaking passionately, I said,

> *If you believe in your peanut potential, if you know you are a diamond, if you are willing to become pearls, then you have the fundamental equipment required to succeed in this class, in this University, and in the larger society. However, as noted in "Equipment," you are the one who must choose your place, you must decide where you want to go, how much you will study the truth to know, and before you return for the next class, you must determine that you have the right equipment. If you don't believe in you, who will? If you don't believe in yourself, I recommend that you drop my class because every-thing I do all term will be based, in part, on you believing in and loving you as much as I do.*

To emphasize the fact that mine was a non-negotiable positive view of them, I ended my lecture by slamming my notebook shut and walking out of the room. The stunned students sat silently in their seats. Ninety-nine percent of my students returned. Some brought friends who desired to take the class, and I signed permission slips for them to do so until the room was at capacity. Years later, many of them still had copies of the poem "Equipment" and had often used it as well as "peanuts, diamonds, and pearls" to motivate young students.

Even Black students who arrived at Pitt with a sense of having the proper "equipment" needed assistance in negotiating the University. Consider, for example, Gil who described his immediate family as "comfortably middle class and rising" at the time that he entered Pitt during the early 1980s. He was also a third generation Pitt student.

Since his father graduated from Pitt and he also had a maternal aunt with a doctorate as well as a paternal aunt with two master's degrees, one would have thought he would easily negotiate the Pitt learning environment. Yet, as a Black student, he noted "...Things can feel so impersonal on a very large urban campus. Having access to the Professor made me feel like I had a harbor, or some place to land..."

Throughout my student days at Pitt, I had no consistent and safe place to land and get refueled, encouraged, and obtain key information I needed to succeed as a student. Therefore, with my classroom and related office hours, I provided safe places for my students to land. When I met with students, I consistently tried to instill in them "the glory of doing the unrequired," a concept borrowed from my home church folk who often told us that God wanted us to not just do what was required, but to also do the "unrequired."

Church Mother Holmes once told me, "If your Mama ask you to scrub the floor, go on and wax the floor even though she didn't ask you to do so." Similarly, my mother often advised her children to not simply perform a task, but instead, "Once a task has begun, never quit it till it's done. Be the task great or small, do it well or not at all." Gil demonstrated the extent to which he internalized this message when he wrote,

> Professor, I will always remember how at times you educated me in subtle, less vocal ways. Certainly, I learned something from all of your lectures. However, there was a deeper level of learning you wanted me and the other students to get. The first class I had with you was Intercultural Communication.

> ...I was feeling pretty good about things when I took the first of your two exams. Out of a possible 100 points, I got 98 points, expecting a pat on the back, or comments on my test like "Very Good!" or "Keep up the good work!" Instead, you wrote, "Unacceptable! You can do better than this." Well, I had mixed emotions about it. ...In time, I came to understand what you were trying to do.

...You drilled into us that we had to do the required and the 'unrequired.' That philosophy helped to raise my standards for the work I'd do for any other professor... Without exception, my work would stand out and the instructor was forced to consider my extra effort. Reports would be typed without error and I would craft charts, graphs, and diagrams to augment my presentations... You provided me and other students one of the strongest weapons against racism: undisputed excellence...

Because so many people had fathers missing from their lives, I can appreciate why they would see you as a father. You have a father's heart and spirit. The Apostle Paul indicated in one of his letters that, "you have many teachers but few fathers." ...You were a pastor because you were a shepherd. What do shepherds do? They seek and provide pasture for the sheep. They also protect the sheep from the destroyer. You were an investor because you invested your time in people who could really give you nothing in return at that time. You were a seer (or see-er) because you walked around campus, taking and keeping the pulse of the students... You were providing shelter from the storms and these things were not part of your job description. You were a catalyst under divine control... How many other stories are going on out there because you were involved in our lives and interceded for us?

As I continued to read through Gil's more than twelve-page correspondence, I was amused by the fact that he was still adhering to the principle of doing the unrequired as opposed to having only sent the few paragraphs I requested. I became more somber when I read the following lines.

Professor, please consider this as you ponder on the lasting impact of your actions with your former students. Did your investments and the quality of those investments have a sustained and fundamental impact on a student's quality of life at the University of Pittsburgh and beyond? I call this the "What If?" factor. What if you had not helped us? Would things have turned out the same for us had you not been involved in our lives? How did your actions and encouragement shape our experience and empower us to overcome the personal, social, historical, and institutional roadblocks to graduating from the University?

I know of no better answer to Gil's "what ifs" than what he wrote himself: "Care and concern were water for us in dry places and, because of you, the small sprouts did not die on the vine." Today, I place the very highest value on having watched so many small sprouts grow into healthy fruits and many of them, in turn, contributed to the healthy growth and development of others as Gil continues to do with his public service program for young men.

Undying love for the students is essential for those who wish to be at the forefront of helping Black students navigated historically White institutions of higher education. The dividends from such motivation will prove to be enormous as was the case with Linda for whom I served as advisor, mentor and sponsor.

When she enrolled at Pitt, Linda benefitted from a program that proactively assisted her and other students with their writing, math and study skills. She was motivated by Black guest speakers of national distinction such as Muhammad Ali. To her benefit, Pitt had started a Black Studies Department and she had taken courses from various Black professors.

Linda enrolled in my Black Rhetoric class and excelled academically. I became a formal advisor for her during her graduate studies during which she produced a thesis and dissertation of the highest quality. By the time she was twenty-five years-old, Linda had earned her baccalaureate, masters, and doctorate from Pitt. Unlike the occasion when I found myself on my own searching for my first faculty position, I introduced Linda and her academic work to leading faculty and administrators responsible for hiring new faculty members. Through such sponsorship and, as was the case with my White graduate student peers, she had interviewed successfully for a position at Howard University before leaving Pitt.

After her career as a Howard University faculty member, Linda held senior administrative positions in the public sector, became chief operating officer of her very successful consulting firm, and subsequently became Chief of Staff for a D.C. public official as well as Director of Communications for the Mayor. Of special importance, in terms of negotiating historically White institutions are the years she spent giving back to Black students via her leadership of Pitt's African American Alumni Association (AAAC).

When I attended Linda's 2006 installation as President of AAAC, I was neither surprised by her bold agenda related to establishing a national organization with regional chapters nor her determination to succeed with a multi-million-dollar scholarship fund to aid Black students at Pitt. Linda had never been the "tamed turkey" described in the following story I often told to my students.

TAMED TURKEYS

Being the oldest child, Marijata often took her younger eagle sibling, Omari, out for flying lessons. One day they flew over a turkey farm and Omari was shocked to see a long line of turkeys marching to the chopping block. Since Marijata seemed to pay them no attention, Omari asked, "Marijata, do you see those turkeys just walking up there to get their heads chopped off? Why don't they do something?" Marijata looked sadly over at Omari and said, "It's useless." Puzzled, Omari pointed out, "Marijata, you and Daddy have always talked to me about becoming a pearl, how we have to agitate some system. Well, why don't we go down there and talk to the turkeys about an action plan?"

Just as Omari began to glide downward, Marijata shouted, "Wait a minute. Let me explain something to you. Last year, I did go down there. I held a secret barnyard meeting. We discussed long term strategies such as learning to fly. We discussed the possibility of just running away at night. We even talked about the possibility of several hundred of them bum rushing the farmer and smothering him. I spent the night with those turkeys and was awakened when the farmer appeared with a shotgun. One of those fools had sneaked off to the farmer, told him what I had been saying, and now the farmer was there to kill me. The farmer had promised to make him an Associate Provost if he pointed me out.

You should have heard the rest of the turkeys telling on me. Fortunately, I got out the back door and flew off. Later that day, I flew over and there they were, getting their heads chopped off." Saddened, Omari asked, "But why were they like that?"

Marijata looked Omari in the eye and said sternly, "Omari, the turkeys are tamed. Tamed turkeys obey their masters, even if it means self-destruction. You must never become tamed!

Not being a "tamed turkey," Linda succeeded in [1] establishing AAAC chapters across the country; [2] getting record numbers of Blacks to become life members of Pitt's alumni association; [3] initiating new programs such as late summer "send offs" whereby Black alumni held receptions for newly admitted Black students in their respective cities; [4] having Pitt partner with the AAAC to implement a successful multi-million dollar campaign to raise scholarships for Black students; and [5] coordinating a 2018–19 University and AAAC sponsored celebration of a half century of diversity progress. In addition, one specific fund, the AAAC Endowed Scholarship Fund, became the largest alumni sponsored endowed fund at Pitt.

After working with Linda for several months on the AAAC agenda, I told her about my writing of this manuscript and asked her to get back to me regarding the Jack she knew when she was a student. Her response included the following:

...As a teacher, Jack was like the spring of life always imparting new words of wisdom and pearls of truths, even when you were

178 | JACK L. DANIEL

not up to hearing any of it. He was your "Mother" conscious about things you had to do right and a thorn about things that you did not do right and knew was wrong. He would admonish as well as defend you... Most of all, he would nurture your mind and not let you forget from whence you came. ...You knew that his love for you was real and predicated on the fact that his mission was to make you intellectually sound and at the same time have you rooted in a healthy self-conscious and in your blackness.

As a teacher, Jack was hard on you, always pushing you beyond your apparent capabilities and beyond where you really wanted to go. The results of that pushing made you a better student and a better person (although it didn't seem that way at the time). With his pushing for excellence (even down to his red markings on your paper that were so vicious it made you think that red ink was the pen color you began with and the original black ink was the markings), you knew deep down he cared and that he was trying to prove something not only to himself but to others.

...his compassion for his students was considered rare by some who didn't really know of his drive and commitment. He would go beyond the call to ensure success for his students.

...Somehow, Jack Daniel knew that in order for his students to succeed, (students who were labeled intellectually marginal and "at-risk" by the establishment's standards), he had to understand what made them "tick," what drove them and what motivated them. His quest, it seemed, led him to solve, mend, or eliminate anything that would get in the way of his student's academic success. It was his personal crusade.

...Jack represented the fall of life as he would harvest his crop (students) and engulf us with his charm, compassion and sensibilities, which was a good way to keep us safe until

time to let us "go ye into all the world." ...Jack believed that I could conquer graduate school when others did not. It was through the insistence of Jack, his belief in my abilities and his encouraging spirit that I learned to write. From my master's thesis to my doctoral dissertation, Jack Daniel propped me up on "every leaning side." He literally drove me to complete graduate studies at age 24 going on age 25 in a few days of graduation.

As a nurturer who had to let go after having planted good seeds and observed those seeds in winter solstice, Jack sent me forth into the highways and byways of life for which I didn't feel comfortable in doing. He pushed me anyway. What a journey. His influence, active involvement and love made the difference...

Black students still need sturdy bridges to help them cross the chasms they encounter in historically White institutions of higher education. They need educational safe havens provided by administrators, scholars, and staff devoted to nurturing them in ways that help them achieve at the highest academic levels. Properly nurtured, Black students will understand and act upon the fact that they have the equipment to fulfill their destinies as "peanuts, diamonds, pearls, and eagles."

Over several decades I had an opportunity to touch many students in small but significant ways and I witnessed them achieve things such as become a state supreme court justice; a member of Congress; a national best-selling author; recipient of a MacArthur Fellowship; distinguished physicians and dentists; major law firm partners; entrepreneurs; top corporate executives; distinguished scholars; and presidents of higher education institutions. Because my freshman experience related to Black professionals was limited to a Black dentist and a Black mortician, I began collecting business cards from my former students. In a few years, I had at least one card from a Black student who had graduated from every major academic unit at Pitt. More than that, so many of them have become "pearls," i.e., activists in social movements as well as helping to advance public policies that benefitted the truly disadvantaged.

My belief in the power of Pitt's Black "pearls" and much of what I aimed to do as a teacher was reinforced when the President of Millersville University, sent me the following March 25, 2008 letter. It is quoted in its entirety because it captured well so much of what I deemed the critically important aspects of my pedagogy.

Dear Jack,

When I think about 1964 and my freshman year at a predominately white university I remember feelings of deep isolation. The university enrolled about 14–17,000 students, of which 50 students might have been black undergraduates. One day, by accident, I wandered into the Tuck Shop (the commuter cafeteria), and there they were – Black people! I was so glad to see them that I remember running toward them.

As I approached the group, I saw a Black male wearing a black coat with a black hat cocked to the side of his head. His outward appearance was that of a man from the "hood". That exterior impression signaled someone who had no serious reason to be at the University. As I moved closer to the group he hollered, "Hey, what's your aim in life?"

I was immediately intimidated and tried to respond with some eloquent statement only to stumble and fumble with an incoherent string of words. I soon learned that this Black man was indeed from the "hood" in Johnstown, PA, but more importantly, was a graduate student. He, like me, was from a working-class family. Based on our family histories, it was not expected that either of us would enroll, not to mention graduate, from a university. His name was Jack Daniel — a wonderful man who asked a life-altering question, came from humble beginnings and went on to earn his doctorate by age 26. As you know, you have been and remain one of my mentors and friends to this day.

I have told the story of meeting you and what subsequently transpired to thousands of students, faculty and staff throughout my 34 years in higher education. I have included this story in two book chapters aimed at helping first year students of color to adjust to college in predominantly white higher education institutions. As you know, I also shared this story at my presidential inauguration at Millersville University.

I have told this story year after year because I felt that it was important for students of color, in particular, to know that ordinary individuals of color make extraordinary contributions to our community, state and world. Furthermore, it is important for them to know that they, too, can achieve; that those who went before them were not born "doctor", "distinguished faculty member" or "president", but achieved those distinctions through persistence, hard work, and disciplined use of their intellect.

My first lesson from you challenged me to think seriously about what I wanted out of life and what goals I wanted to pursue. That life-altering question, "What's your aim in life?" has become my personal compass as I have journeyed through life.

My second "Jack Daniel" lesson would involve the art of research – asking thought-provoking questions that demanded concentration, critical thinking, analysis and, ultimately, action. But first, you had to get my attention. This happened when you served as my advisor for my doctoral program. You had instructed me to draft the first chapter of my dissertation. One bright day I walked into your office with thirteen double-spaced pages of what I judged to be a good draft, an air of confidence and, perhaps, unwarranted arrogance. You looked at the document and placed it in the palm of your hand.

"What is this, you asked in a very calm, but curious, voice. I responded with confidence, "The draft of my first chapter." You looked at me and said, "Mac (You always called me, Mac), I'm not even going to read this. This does not begin to represent your best thinking or work." I was stunned. Not since I had completed my undergraduate degree had anyone questioned the quality of my work. I had modeled my life after you, determined that I would earn no less than an A in every course in which I enrolled. How could you reject my work?

For the next four hours, you asked me question after question, forcing me to think beyond those mere thirteen pages. I found myself having this intense discussion about my topic and delving into the research that I had reviewed. You made me think about the purpose of my research, why the topic was important to me, and what I wanted to accomplish. You were patient with me, but demanded that I think and pushed me to ask myself questions. When I left your office, I was mentally exhausted, certainly less arrogant, and definitely empowered to conduct my research. Ultimately, I began to weave the fabric for my dissertation.

Perhaps my posture when I left that marathon session was not as erect as when I entered, because a few days later I received a special gift from you, a poem entitled "Don't you quit" with a hand-written note, "Francine, Rest if you must, but 'Don't you quit.'" A new lesson full of support – it was okay, even important, to allow myself to stumble, but because of the talents and skills that I possessed, therefore I must persevere.

When my head stopped spinning, I marveled that an Associate Provost could afford to give me that much precious time. Certainly, you had many more things to do that day; things that others would undoubtedly have considered to be "more important." Those four hours produced several more "Jack

Daniel" lessons and became a foundation for how I have sought to live my life.

You taught me that it was, and is, important to give of one's self – to give back. When we give of ourselves to others, when we take time for them, mentor them, support them, invest something of ourselves in them, we touch people as individuals. Some of those individuals then invest themselves in others. The full impact of our investment may never be known to us because there is an exponential quality to it. Quantifying the return on our investment isn't important; making the investment, you taught me, is what is important.

You further taught me that "getting by" was unacceptable and that anyone can perform in a mediocre manner. More importantly, if one is determined to reach their aim in life, it requires fortitude, strength, and a support system to go the extra miles. I learned to expect the best from myself in order to set that same expectation for others. I learned that there was more depth inside me than I realized, but that it was up to me to plumb that depth. I learned to ask those penetrating questions of myself, my students and of those with whom I work.

I would be remiss if I did not acknowledge the content and knowledge that I gained from the course work that you assigned to me. For the first time in my life, I had an instructor who was knowledgeable about my culture. The scholarship by African Americans to which I was introduced was empowering and exciting. Imagine learning about the range of Black communication which included, but was not limited, to sociological, psychological, anthropological, scientific, historical, religious and musical aspects. Realizing that I only scratched the surface of this knowledge during my doctoral studies provided an incentive to continue my education about these outstanding contributions. Being introduced to these scholars by you, who dared to excel as a scholar in this field, was a gift, as was the lesson that learning is a life-long pursuit.

Throughout my doctoral studies, you periodically would send other poetry gifts. One that has remained my favorite is entitled, "Equipment." This poem teaches all who read it that they have the equipment to conquer the world if they will utilize their God-given talents. What a powerful poem! From the time I began my career as a faculty member and psychological counselor, to this day, I have worked to give back to my students what you gave to me. I read "The Equipment" poem to all my freshmen because I want them to excel beyond their wildest imaginations. I feel compelled to share my personal story that includes Jack Daniel because I want others to stretch themselves and to refuse to accept mediocrity within themselves.

What I learned most from you was to reach for my aim in life. My aim in life -- to spread a little of Jack Daniel and myself to all my students. You have made a tremendous impact on my life, not just by how you taught, but BECAUSE you taught -- by your actions, your penetrating questions and your infinite collection of encouraging poetry. I had the opportunity to witness your transformation through several roles: graduate student, faculty member, administrator of the Black Studies Department, ACE Fellow, and ultimately the Vice Provost and Dean at the University of Pittsburgh. You were and are my role model for you dared to travel the road less traveled for African Americans during the past four decades.

Sincerely,
Francine (Mac)

It is very important to note that Francine sprang from the soil of Pittsburgh's Hill District which continues to be one of Pittsburgh's most distressed communities. She demonstrated clearly what can happen when barriers to achievement are removed and essential assistance is provided for negotiating historically White university community. In her case, she not only did so at Pitt but soared in eagle-like fashion to negotiate successfully in other historically White universities by serving as [1] a tenured faculty member and subsequently Dean of Academic Support Services and Assistant to the Vice President for Academic Affairs at Clarion University; [2] Associate Provost at West Chester University; and [3] Provost and Vice President for Academic Affairs before serving as President of Millersville University. If we are to have ongoing success stories such as Francine's, then historically White universities' faculty and administrators must undertake the following charge.

Key members of the historically White university must hold a deep and abiding sense of responsibility similar to that contained in Charles Wesly's hymn, "A Charge to Keep I Have." As C. Michael Hawn wrote, "This hymn is an unequivocal call to commitment to follow the Master and to fulfill our vocation through service. Part of the second stanza states, "to serve the present age, my calling to fulfill…"

Operating with "a charge to keep I have," a wide array of faculty members must provide our students with "safe places to land." To do so, faculty members must first and foremost be steeped in "undying love" for their students –all of them regardless of race, gender and other demographic factors. Secondly, they must abide by the belief that their students have unlimited growth potential, that as Carver did with the peanuts, it is the faculty members' duty to help draw out the many possibilities that are within the students.

In keeping their charge, faculty members must have the highest expectations for their students and, simultaneously, do their parts in helping students have the highest expectations for themselves. They must understand the cognitive as well as cultural "equipment" their students bring to their classrooms. By doing things such as I did when I constantly pushed my students to do the "glory of the unrequired," caused them to think about their "aims in life" and how to achieve them, and listened as well as talked with them in the safety of my office or sometimes while walking across campus, faculty members can learn what their students can do with and without help and, in turn, what they must do to help their students soar as high as "eagles."

As faculty members undertake their charge, administrators must insure that students function in a learning community that is unfettered by racism, sexism, homophobia, xenophobia, religious bias, and other forms of inhumanity on the rise in 2018. They must take the lead and ultimate responsibility in transforming their historically White universities into truly diverse and inclusive institutions. They must make sure that their tuition rates are not so high that students are economically disenfranchised from enrolling.

Black students must appreciate in no uncertain terms what James Baldwin meant when he said, "Our crown has already been bought and paid for. All we have to do is wear it." In the case of Pitt, they must appreciate the fact that over the last half century, Black students, faculty and administrators along with others have paid the price for them to enroll and succeed at Pitt. Now that the door of opportunity is open, as my mother often said, they must be prepared to walk through and do all that they can to succeed at the highest levels. If they fulfill their charge, then truly they will become free and, in turn, give back to those who come after them.

‡

— This is a work of creative nonfiction. It is my recall and analysis of key episodes during my time as a student, faculty member and administrator at the University of Pittsburgh. In some instances, names and background scenes have been changed.

I thank those who took the time to read **Negotiating a Historically White University while Black**. *Millions of people continue to negotiate their ways through places they were previously excluded on the basis of their race, religion, sexuality, gender, nationality, or other demographic factors. As such, it is very important that there be mutual support among those advancing diversity, inclusion, equity and social justice. Pursuant to this agenda, I serve as a Contributor for the* **Pittsburgh Urban Media** *which describes itself as follows: "Launched in August 2009,* **Pittsburgh Urban Media** *is an online magazine that connects visitors to the diverse communities in Pittsburgh and the surrounding neighborhoods. Our online magazine showcases the people, places and things that make Pittsburgh one of the most livable cities in the United States."*

http://www.pittsburghurbanmedia.com/

Concerned with the ongoing threats associated with Black males' ability to successfully proceed from childhood to manhood to fatherhood, I co-authored with my son, Omari C. Daniel, **We Fish, the Journey to Fatherhood** *(University of Pittsburgh Press, 2003). Therein, we discuss keys to doing so. See:*

https://www.amazon.com/We-Fish-Fatherhood-Jack-Daniel-ebook/dp/ B005ZELFH8

Those who wish to follow-up on matters pertaining to **Negotiating a Historically White University while Black**, *can reach me at:*

jackldaniel@comcast.net
danielj@pitt.edu
Facebook@JLD4442

Jack L. Daniel

30784947R00104

Made in the USA
San Bernardino, CA
29 March 2019